ONCE WE HAD A COUNTRY

Jack Alster

Once we had a Country

Cover: Panorama of central Vienna looking towards Stefansdom (St Stephen's Cathedral) by courtesy of Austrian National Tourist Office. Art work by Advertising Print Ltd., Wetherby.

Able Publishing

13 Station Road, Knebworth, Herts SG3 6AP

Tel: 01438 812320/814316 Fax: 01438 815232

www.ablepublishing.co.uk
email: fp@ablepublishing.co.uk

ISBN 1 903607 15 7

This book is dedicated to the memory of my dear mother, Stella Alster

Acknowledgements

Two people have nurtured this book from start to finish: my wife, Ann, and the poet Edward Storey (author of Fen-boy First). I cannot thank them enough for their unstinting help and continuous enthusiasm. I would also like to thank James Moore (Cambridge lecturer in short stories) for applying his fine critical mind and giving me unfailing support. Hugh Douglas (biographer and historian) was responsible for getting this work into print, and Steve Hammond was the one whose enthusiastic support got me started on the project. Big thanks to both.

The creative writing groups of Peterborough (Tutor, June Counsel), March and Doddington and Cambridge gave me the opportunity of reading out my work and providing invaluable feedback. Also thanks to my typist, Jane Bentley, for her hard work and helpfulness.

Lastly, I would like to thank the humane official who turned a blind eye to allow me to enter England. This book also expresses my gratitude to all those who helped me to find a new country.

Contents

Introduction

Part 1 – THE FAMILY

Chapter 1	Dad	11
Chapter 2	Old & New	17
Chapter 3	Siggy	22

Part 2 – THE ANSCHLUSS

Chapter 4	The Nazis arrive	33
Chapter 5	The Long Wait	39
Chapter 6	A Horror	42
Chapter 7	Robert	43
Chapter 8	The Chase	49
Chapter 9	Kristallnacht	52
Chapter 10	Goodbye Vienna	54

Part 3 – ENGLAND, OH ENGLAND

Chapter 11	A Nazi in Hampstead	59
Chapter 12	Dotheboys Hall	65
Chapter 13	The Tulip	67
Chapter 14	Nearly a Catholic	71
Chapter 15	Little Austria	76
Chapter 16	Mrs Adams	79
Chapter 17	The Coopers	84
Chapter 18	Escape from Wem	92
Chapter 19	Mr Rowley	100
Chapter 20	My Bomb	107
Chapter 21	Uncle	111
Chapter 22	Marianne	120
Chapter 23	Finding Father	126

Illustrations

Mother	Dedication page
Father	16
Nothing to Smile About - picture of the family	29
Jews forced to scrub pavements	38
Mother and Son / An English schoolboy	70
Graduation Day	129
Father in New York	130

Introduction

I remember the ghetto in Vienna with affection. The twisty streets were cobbled so cars were rarely seen and children could cross the road with safety. There were ice carts with huge horses slipping on the cobbles, and the occasional trader trundling his wares. This was my world. This was where everyone lived who mattered to me: mum, dad, aunts, uncles, cousins – all warm, energetic and neurotic, ready to look after me and cosset me.

Some of the younger people had left the ghetto for the suburbs. But we were still there, amongst the warmth, the chaos and the poverty.

Part 1

THE FAMILY

Chapter 1

Dad

I was eight, lost in the confusion of two angry lives.

The tiny kitchen was the focus. I'm sure its smallness added to the tension, for all wild words were spoken in there. A large wooden table took up half the kitchen's space, and one chair in particular was memorable for it was so out of place in the kitchen – a mahogany chair with beautiful legs. And now comes the vision of visions – one leg was completely broken and pure white splinters stuck up nastily at me. I stared at the splinters, fascinated; it was a wounded chair, broken by a man's anger. The man was there now, panting; he was huge, he was a shadow to my right, but I wasn't afraid of him for I sensed he was bewildered by the strength of anger that had done this deed – a man stopped in the midst of rage and now appalled at what had happened.

To my left was the other person – so thin, so vulnerable, withdrawn in fright to the comfort of the wall; and as I stared at her liquid brown eyes, I saw a strange light in them – the light of triumph, for she had conquered by tempting the man into the unpardonable deed – his use of brute force. So now it was he who was helpless, lost in confusion – trying, in his own way, to return to the comfort of ordinary behaviour. So baffled was he that he swayed. I cringed for I was in the middle: would anger in its blind stupefying way turn on me? I looked at his large hands, but they had never struck me in anger, in fact, images of his hands were of their fumbling clumsily with tiny nuts on my meccano set or hands reaching out to stroke my straight hair, hands of benediction, of comfort.

He spoke throatily to the woman:

"I'll give you some money next week – I swear to you – !"

He looked appealingly at her but saw only doubting eyes. The deed had been done, the chair was there as evidence, there could be no forgiveness. So he turned and I heard him walk quickly through the small hall and bang the front-door so hard the flat vibrated.

After he'd gone she made no direct appeal to me – no great hugs and tears; she began to move things about mechanically and asked wearily: "Do you want supper – it's spinach and egg?"

* * * * *

"At least now we'll have some peace." Did I say that? Or did she invent it to justify the break-up? "See," I heard her tell the whole wide world: "Jackie is with me – he's on my side, all he wants is peace." I didn't contradict, for here was a partial truth – my longing for that dependable ordinariness that is the ideal background to a child's life: the pillars of habit, of egg and spinach for supper, of retreating to my room where meccano bits gave shape to wild imaginings – these pillars were what she tried so hard to re-establish, and she succeeded – except now there was a hole in our lives, a huge gaping hole.

Of course neither of us spoke of it: no mention of dad, instead she covered me with love and over-did it, her caresses becoming embarrassing. Only my favourite foods were served up: dumpling soup, buttered liver, chocolate ice-cream, and, on Sundays, schnitzel – undercooked, but I praised it for I saw it as the well-meant effort of the incompetent. "Nice this," I said, and received a warm smile of gratitude.

Routine was her ally, for children fit easily into grooves of habit. Meanwhile memory was shelved. Did the image of dad undergo a subtle change as it sank lower and lower in my mind? I'm not sure, though I sensed a softening at the edges as imagination became servant to the wish to get him back. Not that I knew how, or ever asked: "Where's he gone?" or "Will he ever come back to us?" no, silence had clamped down on the subject through a kind of mutual embarrassment, though one day there came a shock as I opened his wardrobe and it was completely bare with two swaying coathangers – here was direct evidence of a ghost that had fled.

Strangely, I didn't sense danger in Egon's sudden appearance in our kitchen. He was not a relative, but suddenly he was there, an unexplained stranger, who sat in the shadow, a perpetual smile on his face and vanishing as soon as he decently could on my return from school.

"Got to go … Byeeeee …"

It was obvious he was in a different category from others, for, apart from mum telling me he was a 'friend', she never talked about him as, for instance, we chatted about Aunt Irma or Uncle Henry, who now came more frequently for visits. Since dad's departure we'd become much more sociable, there was even an unacknowledged 'visitors' corner in the kitchen, and I enjoyed the noise and bustle and was relieved at the lessening pressure of mum's personality on my affairs. Now I could retreat, without guilt, into my sanctuary from which I could watch, down below, the Jewish scene – less ostentatiously 'Jewish' now the Seyss-Inquart Austrian Nazis were active – no black and white shawls and rarely a Kippah. It was my window on life and it was there that Egon suddenly and dramatically impinged himself on my mind, for, by pure chance, we met outside the large green front door leading to the flats – he leaving the place, I coming home. "Why Jackie!" he opened his arms in surprise and smiled, "Hello!" and one hand reached towards me to shake. But I ignored it, I walked round it; I stared up at him, a broken half-smile on my face, and rushed past him into the dark comfort of the flats. My heart was thumping. Why? Surely it was an ordinary enough meeting; but now, I knew it wasn't – I'd rejected him and was glad. He'd wanted me to like him but I'd turned him down – my 'liking' wasn't to be bought as easily as that – no, I'd make him pay for it – dearly.

I raced up the stairs and there the door to our flat was open and there stood mum, fury on her face.

"How *could* you!"

"What?"

"You know 'what'. Get in here!" and she half dragged me into the hall. I was all innocence: "What have *I* done?"

"You know very well what you've done," and she shouted, "He wants to be your friend!"

Pretence was useless for she must have been watching from the window. Now she was bending down, staring into my face.

"Manners, Jackie, manners," and she prodded me towards the kitchen.

"I've taught you manners (prod) and you've let me down (prod). What have you got against him? Go on – tell me!"

"Nothing."

"Why didn't you shake his hand then?"

I didn't answer: excuses were useless, explanations beyond me. She persisted: "Go on, why didn't you – all you had to do was take his hand!" Now her face was very, very close, and, driven by instinct, I riposted: "Where's dad?" It was more accusation than question. She straightened up. I saw her blush; I saw guilt, regret, doubt – all go across her face, and then, barely audibly, she mumbled:

"With Rosa."

"What?"

"You heard: With Rosa – "

"Who's Rosa?"

She shouted: "Oh, for God's sake, she's his girl-friend!" And she turned away and went into the kitchen and began mechanically moving things about as she did when things got on top of her. I followed, desperately hoping there'd be no tears – anything but that! But one question had to be asked: "Is he never coming back?"

She didn't answer.

I repeated: "Mum, is he never – ?" And she yelled: "I DON'T KNOW! I JUST DON'T KNOW!" There was a short pause, and then, in an almost normal voice, she said: "Go and change your school clothes." And, with relief, I escaped.

I always thought he'd come back, I realised that now. The shock that he mightn't left me stunned. I stared out of my window as though summoning the outside world for help, and saw ordinary life as ordinary as ever: Klapholz – the second-hand clothes dealer. Mrs Schumann and her perpetual kids, and a young Jew brave enough to wear a Kippah in these Nazi-ridden times.

I thought: Dad gone, dad a vanishing figure, dad, desirable even in his rages, leaving me alone. In comparison Egon seemed ridiculous – so slight and so boyish. The two men were absurdly different – dad with his lion-like mane of grey hair, his strong features and noble look seemed to give Egon no chance at all. I decided there was no contest, and felt, not only a glow of loyalty, but the comfort of a foregone conclusion.

* * * * *

She came to me with a shy smile: if I wanted, next week-end, I could stay with dad and *'Aunt'* Rosa. Too many emotions sometimes strike you dumb – yes, I was eager, but, above all, I was embarrassed – to meet Rosa and dad *together* in a strange place! But, of course, I agreed.

Their place was full of light and bustle. The main room – the 'food' room – was cheerful with a large window, and dad, eager to put me at ease, showed me how to sharpen a pencil over the sink, how to play chess, he said: "Yum, yum," as he swallowed almost whole soft sultana pancakes – his grey hair piled up magnificently, with sweat stains under his arm-pits, and there was Rosa as well!

She wasn't what I expected, she was *more* than I expected – she – a large, very dark woman, with contrasting freckles – was shy of me. *She* shy of *me*! Oh dear, oh dear, my shyness was so extreme it stopped all words. Nor could I look her in the eyes – for, young as I was, I sensed the awesome power of an overwhelming sexuality. I couldn't handle it – I was bewildered by it – totally thrown – I couldn't even look at her large body so disturbing was its impact. That we slept in the same bed (dad in the middle) even now makes me tingle; and there remains one pre-eminent image – of a long black hair on her calf – I daren't raise my eyes higher as she undressed unashamedly in front of me.

This interlude in heaven had stilled my worst fears, for, if dad hadn't come home, neither had he disappeared. He was *there*, only about half a mile away – and now seemed to me an even more glamorous figure than before. Unwittingly, he had opened a new door of life to me – for, on return to the gloom of our flat, I felt the prick of tears – I had had *too* good a time. Mum looked anxiously at me, tried to hug me – something not welcomed but borne with good grace. She sensed I preferred the 'other' place – she was hurt and I couldn't bear this. Not her fault we lived in this miserable cramped flat, which, in the evening, before bed, was so silent, so dead, so very lonely – even Egon might have been welcomed at that point.

But, hard as she tried, mother couldn't bring 'life' to our lonely flat. I was no companion for her and her moods affected me badly; frankly, we got on each other's nerves. So, it was a blessing that, as she had to go out to work full-time now, relatives looked after me.

Father, cigar in hand as usual, apparently well in Italian prison camp.

Chapter 2

Old & New

There were only two rooms that mattered to me in Aunt Anna's flat – Uncle David's and his son's, Norbert. True, the flat contained three rooms, but Aunt Anna's kitchen didn't really count in my imagination. Curious, really, for I spent much of my time there, especially when she was making Apfelstrudel. I'd watch fascinated as she carefully made the dough: exact amount of flour, always two eggs and a precise amount of milk. Then came the stirring and soon I'd come into my own as the dough thickened into a yellow gummy blob from which she'd neatly cut off a small slice and give it to me to make dough animals. But the animals only half absorbed me as her thick thumb anchored the dough on one corner of the large table and then came the breath-taking thrill of stretching it to cover the whole table. Careful, careful, for at any moment a hole – however tiny – might appear, and then, with a heartfelt 'Oh, dear God!', she'd have to bundle it all together, pummel it, dust it with flour and start all over again. The resultant meal, however, came from heaven – thick bloody beetroot slices, thin sliced gherkins, and, at the end, the Apfelstrudel always leaving runs of sugary fat down my chin.

Meanwhile, uncle David had his meal in his own room down the corridor on a tray carried by aunt making her one daily call on her spouse; and, straining my ears as hard as I could, I never heard a word pass between them – just the click of his door as he remained a recluse. I was the emissary between the kitchen with its life and light and the deep gloom of uncle David's place. I entered without knocking for I was 'at home' here. I would sit just below eye-level and stare up at the Singer sewing machine and the black figure which sat by it – always staring, with eyes never clear for a film of liquid always covered them – ready for tears which never came. I faced the room's only source of light – a small square window divided into quarters with dirty, begrimed glass, and, as its dim light fell on Rembrandt-like machine and man, we would simply sit and sit. If impatience nagged me, it soon went for the ancient figure created the calm of eternity. No conversation, but, every now and then, very suddenly, he'd press the pedal, the machine would whirr, and, with trembling hands, he'd guide a piece of thin cloth through the twin steel prongs and out came a line of stitches. He never finished an article in my presence for energy having spilled out of him for a few seconds would soon give out and he'd resume his sitting and staring. My ears would strain for signs of life from outside and celebrate a screaming jolting tram making its way through Vienna's mid-day slumber and I'd think of those millions outside, dulled by heat, perhaps, like uncle and myself, lost in dreams.

Why did I love him when there was so much to disgust me? There was the po – an object to his right, thank heaven, covered by a patterned cloth, and to his left the fascinating spittoon – the idea of his using it and allowing me to see if the phlegm would hit or miss would be a dramatic highlight in our sojourn. (He never did.)

Perhaps it was his peace, perhaps it was the fact that he tolerated me but made no demands, perhaps there's simply something very calming and peaceful in extreme old age that reached beyond the call of the nervous vibrancy that was me.

Anyway, love him I did for he was the restful peace amidst turbulence, and, besides, even without conversation, propinquity creates curious bonds. This scarcely-breathing dark figure with its black kippah became an icon in my imagination – the real Jew, the eternal Jew – the symbol of a dark but beloved history.

Soon my eyes would droop; the machine, man and window would become a blur and I knew it was time for me to enter another world next door, the world of Norbert where I was allowed to rest on his delightful bed.

Only a wall separated father and son's rooms, but what an aggressive rejection was one of the other! Art Deco dominated this place with its clean light green walls; the low bed was pine with a startling red and blue Dada design on the cover. On the central table were rolls of architectural blueprints surrounded by the neat gadgetry of large important-looking set-squares and immaculate steel angle measurers. However, my focus was a still-life of three green apples produced by the talented Norbert – an oil painting vibrant with the juicy roundness of green fruit. Having entered the room feeling drowsy, I was soon aroused by the assault on my senses, by the call of the twentieth century, by youth and success. Never did I get tired of the white drawings on the blueprints; so mathematically correct, to the precise millimetre, a challenge for me to copy. But my copying was transgressing a hidden law: this is Norbert's room – don't disturb! Here the son had carved out for himself a sanctuary of modernity, made a statement: 'I am different!' Here, looking, lounging, but rarely still for long, I'd dream dreams of ambition, of joining an optimistic forward-looking set who knew no boundaries – all drawn by the strident promise of the modern world.

Then, one day, aunt Anna said she couldn't deal with me just now – she was busy; also, on no account was I to go into Norbert's room.

"Why not?"

"Ah," she said mysteriously, but smiling, and I noticed she was wearing a new light grey dress that was intending to say: 'Today is special!' but merely made her look impossibly fat. She was bustling, she was nervous:

"Just go away and do something," she said. Wounded, I went into uncle David's room, which, at first, seemed much as usual, though even he was more active and actually buzzed away at his machine with some vigour. For a change he turned over his eternal piece of cloth and began another; also, and this was startling, he had shaved; his cheeks looked red raw and uncomfortable and he wore a tie – not much of a tie – a black one – but still a tie. What on earth was going on, and suddenly, also startling, he said: "Norbert – Norbert's coming!" and his cracked old face looked almost ecstatic.

"Doesn't he live here?" I asked, astonished.

"Got his own place now," uncle David mumbled, "But today – !" and he looked into the distance, and then – would there be no end to the day's surprises – I saw the room was lighter – the window had been cleaned. I looked round and saw – albeit dimly – uncle David's bed and an old armchair, both usually out of sight in the gloom.

I also got excited as the parents' agitation transmitted itself to me. The great architect was coming, the son on whom all their hopes were pinned – the owner of the magic room!

But the time of his anticipated coming came and went. Norbert had not appeared. Aunt Anna began to walk up and down the corridor, looking out of the windows to see when her darling would appear. Uncle David got up once or twice and then suddenly told me to "Get out!". I knew he wanted to use the po. I didn't know where to go and looked longingly at Norbert's room. Had that been changed as well? Perhaps been decorated in a new way? And, at last, the sound of heavy footsteps were heard coming up to the flat.

Into uncle's room aunt shoved me as though Norbert was to be seen by no-one but her – thank heaven uncle David had had time to finish his toilet. As I heard (but didn't see) Norbert greet his mum, uncle David got so agitated I began to get worried. He went to the door, hesitated, and came back again. They went, very fast, past the window, mother and son, and into the kitchen – talking -.

'Why doesn't he go and join them?' I wondered, but some shyness, some inhibition seemed to stop him as though he was forever consigned to his room. He began to pace round nervously. He re-made his bed and patted the duvet just for something to do. He sat at the sewing machine but couldn't bring himself to start it up. Of course I itched to go and see the great man, but thought – there'll be time enough. And from the kitchen came laughter – it was aunt Anna's but it sounded like a young woman's – a totally happy laugh. I heard the two of them come along the corridor – would they visit us now? But no, they went into Norbert's room. Surprisingly, I could hear them fairly clearly through the thick wall. A cupboard door opened – "Remember -?" asked aunt and I heard a deep rumble from Norbert – he had a rich mature man's voice. The cupboard door closed and they laughed again and then silence except for a sniffle from aunt Anna and some mumbled intimacies I couldn't pick up. Suddenly "Sorry – can't stop," from Norbert and I all but sensed aunt Anna's pain. Silence – perhaps a kiss and a hug? "Soon – soon?" asked aunt Anna. A blur and Norbert flashed past the window.

"Bye dad!" he called quite cheerfully, "Can't stop," but didn't come in.

Uncle David moved surprisingly quickly, went to the door, opened it, raised his hand in salutation and then lowered it as the front door banged shut.

The pathos of that hand lowered was too much for me. I felt the prick of tears. I saw uncle David turn round and look hopelessly beyond me into the room's dark.

He stood humiliated, defeated, in the middle, appearing not to know what to do. Then slowly he went back to the machine, sat down and mechanically he pressed the pedal, the whirr began; he tried to guide the cloth but it concertinad together, the material had gone too fast for his withered hands. He stopped and sat and sat ....

I looked anxiously at him, at the raw red folds on his neck, at the unaccustomed tie and saw, silently, perhaps not wishing to embarrass me, that he was crying ...

Chapter 3

Siggy

Remembering Norbert's thoughtlessness towards his father left me bewildered. Even as a child I felt the indignation of witnessing injustice and not being able to do anything about it. In the case of Uncle Siggy, who lived just down the street from us, I knew a greater sense of helplessness for polio had struck him down in 1910 and reshaped his whole life. My ever-present image of him is of an arm raised awkwardly so that his elbow could get under the shiny brown strap which went down from his shoulder into that mysterious area somewhere near his legs. I never saw his legs, so buckled and twisted were they and so ashamed was he of them. Perhaps when I was watching, his legs were pushed sideways so I couldn't see them. But I knew he worked his legs by moving his shoulders and somehow got his dead limbs over the ridge of his wheelchair where he settled down for the day never to move his legs again till the shoulders raised them. He was a living marionette.

Apart from the completely twisted body and dead legs, he was all bones. His head (except for the marvellous brown eyes) was a skull with tight skin on; he had a high rather noble forehead and then the head caved backwards as if in retreat. There were virtually no lips and his cheeks were hollowed out; the neck was skinny – an old man's (though he could only have been around 30) and then came startling perpendicular shoulders which descended, like an inverted triangle, into the rest of his misshapen body, from which, even I, at 8, averted my eyes.

When mother said: "Uncle Siggy will look after you when I'm at work," I almost, but not quite, cried out an objection. "You don't mind, do you?" she persisted. I'd turned my head away. It wasn't lack of affection for Uncle Siggy, but the aversion children have of the diseased.

I didn't argue with mother – we were so close (after my father left) that emotion was transmitted by telepathy. She knew I didn't want to go to that room on the 3rd floor in one of Vienna's poorer districts where Uncle Siggy slept and worked, but she couldn't deal with my reluctance: she had enough to worry about with work and making ends meet without caring over-much about my feelings – they had to take a back-seat.

The odd thing was I did feel a sort of sympathy for Uncle Siggy because I was often ill myself, but sympathy is one thing, being with him for hours on end is another.

Now I realise he was as reluctant as I. In fact, when I was left by mother in his one large room, he looked nervously at me. "I've got some books for you," he said eagerly, "I've also got your favourite chocolate balls." Why didn't I smile at him, why didn't I have the heart to see an adult making desperate efforts to 'get on' with a child? Because a child (anyway, this child) had a rather priggish honesty: I saw the long day stretching ahead without much talk and within the claustrophobia of one adult and one child, and foresaw only tedium in a hot room and frustration which might well lead to tantrums and temper. Worse, temper which had to be suppressed, for Uncle Siggy was the family victim: the poor soul who had been dealt some lousy cards by life and who – I was constantly warned – must always be treated kindly, even pitied. So tantrums were out.

The books meant nothing: few pictures and indecipherable writing – a blur of print I had no intention of even attempting, for, much more interesting, at the other end of his large thick work table, were a glitter of jeweller's instruments, especially the electric cleaning wheel, the dentist-like cutting drill, the immaculate leather-shiny cloths, and a whole range of boxes – all cardboard except one – a black metal box with a lock on it. I guessed that's where he kept *real* gems – the immensely valuable diamonds and rubies and sapphires and emeralds.

I couldn't wait to see those colours in twinkling flashes be worked by him. Impatiently I waited for him to start. He clicked – here we could be together – here our interests would coincide! So, with a sly grin, he unlocked the box and there were little light brown envelopes, all marked, and he took one out – his hands were surprisingly steady – and, very carefully, he spilled out five diamonds.

He sighed and glowed at me: "These," he pointed, "are absolutely beautiful!"

I was disappointed – no colours!

"What about – ?" I pointed to the others.

"Ah, you like colours – but they're not so valuable."

"Can I see?"

And slowly, like exposing Aladdin's cave, he rolled out a few rubies, a few sapphires, a few emeralds.

"What if they fall in the holes?" The table was pitted with hundreds of holes made by cutting instruments, holes that were black with dirt and some looking very deep.

"They won't," he said, "because I won't let them."

"But what if they *do*?"

"Then I'd have to cut the table to bits to get them out," and he took from his rack a steel-shiny chisel which, to this day, I can see glinting in the sunlight with its razor sharpness.

"Cut, cut, cut," he said, miming the action. "If I lose one of these –," he stopped, not daring to speculate – it was too horrible to think of. So – as if the event was about to happen – he carefully returned most of the stones to their envelopes, closed the sacred box and locked it. A few stones were left out.

"Now read!" he commanded, and, ignoring me, got to work. He was a transformed man at his job: the bony fingers would flicker like things possessed, the ring put delicately into the tiny blue vice, the eye-glass put on his right eye and then came the rasp of cutting – slight rasps, longer rasps, always followed by a look of judgement. He picked up each stone with a sucking tube and inserted it precisely into the hole in the ring.

"Those are valuable?" I asked.

"Very – but never mind those. Here –," and he got out one of the other boxes and spilled out an orgy of coloured stones on to the table. "You can play with those."

"All of them?"

"All of them," he smiled.

"What about your stones – the ones you're working?"

"What about them?"

"They're special?"
"They certainly are."
"Who are they for?"
"A lady."
"Is she pretty?"
"Ah –" and his smile turned into a sort of glow – "she's rather – " he picked his word carefully – "attractive." But I sensed that this "attractive lady" was not a wife or a girlfriend and that Uncle Siggy would never have either, nor would he have children – he was the sort of person who made you cry when you think of him. But, I decided, when dinner came along and he carefully presented me with my ration of one chocolate ball, he was really OK.

The day had presented me with a myriad of images, but it was the five diamonds, lying innocently on the work-bench, that stayed with me most vividly.

On Siggy's small wireless we heard that Hitler was making more and more strident demands that Austria should join the 'Great German Reich'. The Austrian government's feeble response was 'we will review the situation'. For us Jews the coming of the Germans would, of course, be a disaster. I was vaguely aware of this, but not sure of it all.

"What's happening?" I asked.

But mother and Siggy ignored me; so, cocooned by ignorance and bored by what I didn't quite understand, I began to play with the cheap stones Siggy had given me as toys. I arranged them in two lines: one paste diamonds, the other coloured.

"The German army," I pointed, "And the Austrian army". I moved a coloured (Austrian) one up and shot down one German 'diamond', and then another and another until the German army was vanquished, and, mentally, I raised the red-white-red flag of Austria in triumph.

Suddenly, and catching me completely unawares, arms were around me and mother's familiar odour engulfed me, tears dropped on my shoulders, her hair entangled with mine. I couldn't bear these impulsive outbursts of hers. I knew she was upset and trying to take comfort from me, and knew my love should respond to hers – it was my duty. But I shrank away, she retreated and looked at me, hurt. I turned away from all this emotion and rushed back to my stones. They had become 'my' world – more real than the real world, more amenable to my wishes, much easier to understand.

On that day, after mother left, Siggy, to my relief, said nothing. he returned to his work, and, once there, he was, like me, totally engrossed. We were companions in evasion; here, in our tiny world, the Germans could go to the devil and leave us in peace.

It was Siggy's unconcern about a German invasion that made his large, sunny room so attractive. He was different from my other uncles and aunts who had become so nervous about the political situation that I shunned them. However, Siggy was immune to all this. He worked his rings, he carved stones of immense beauty, he put on his straps, and every day he gave me a chocolate ball, and, even better, began to take an interest in my games. "Nazis and Jews," I pointed to my 'army' lines that had now changed character.

"And who wins?" he asked, smiling.

"The Jews!"

"Of course," he said, and went on with his work. I now sensed a mutual affection for we had lost all self-consciousness. We were companions in that sunny room, having excluded the world in what was now almost my home.

If Uncle Siggy was calmer than my other relations it was because if the Germans came he had no hope of escape – he knew that no country in the world would take him in his condition, and that gave him a sort of peace. But one day I realised it was a superficial peace, for suddenly we heard Seyss-Inquart's Nazi gangs[1] singing the Horst Wessel song not far from our house. He stopped to listen, as I did. Then I rushed to the window to look. "Get back!" he shouted and he was surprisingly harsh. I stared at him and his magnificent eyes were filled with hate. It scared me for he always seemed a person of gentle emotions. I saw his hands trembling and realised he was as frightened as I. When the song faded, he called me to him. He looked straight into me. "Sorry," he said, "Sorry I spoke harshly – but never – *never* watch!" Then in a more sympathetic voice: "Were you frightened?" I nodded, and then, suddenly, as impulsively as mother, he embraced me. I smelt his smell – different and sweaty, I also found my legs caught between his dead ones and my body crushed to his bony breast.

I felt his straps, his hot shirt and some metal plate. He kissed my head, once, twice, and, when I looked up, he'd turned his head away to hide his tears. The emotion was too much for me – I'd never as much as touched him before, or he me. I recoiled, and, desperately trying to hide my revulsion, went to my stones for sanctuary. He returned to his work, and, for a while, only the rasping of worked stones broke the silence. But then, suddenly, he turned away from the bench, and, moving his wheel-chair very fast, he retreated behind the flimsy, grey curtain that separated his bed from the rest of the room. I heard the clanking of a pail and knew he was about to do his toilet but had forgotten to tell me to leave the room and wait outside in the corridor. I looked at my stones for distraction, arranged them in familiar lines and then suddenly noticed that, in his hurry, he'd left the real diamond packet out and four of them were lying temptingly near the vice. With the devil in me, I switched one diamond for one of my paste ones – they looked indistinguishable, and, just as I was doing this, he swished the curtain back, and, in my confusion, the real diamond dropped into one of the holes and disappeared. As he came back in his chair, I stared in horror at the hole and my vision blurred and I couldn't remember which hole it was. Apparently he'd noticed none of this. He returned to work and clicked on the cleaning wheel while I tried to force my mind to remember *which* hole, but they seemed like a pitted moon-scape, one hole like the other. I comforted myself, thinking no one will know – mock diamonds are like real ones; once they're polished only experts can tell.

It took two days for retribution to come and it was the worst kind. I could stand harsh words, even slaps, I could stand mother's not infrequent hysteria, but what happened was two adults looking at me with doleful, puzzled looks of "How could you!"

"Why?" asked mother, "Why?"

I had no answer, but sensed that Uncle Siggy understood and the understanding made it worse – I think he knew how unwelcome his embrace had been, he knew the toilet bit, but what hurt was that perhaps he thought I didn't like him and had taken a very nasty revenge.

"Give it here!" mother held out her hand.

"Haven't got it."

She paled.

"Then where -?" I pointed vaguely at the pitted table. "It dropped down there."

"Where – whereabout?" There was panic. She stroked the table, tried to put her fingers down the holes but couldn't get them in.

"I don't know!" I shouted, "Just about here – " and drew a circle that included about 50 holes.

Uncle Siggy looked at the spot as though willing the diamond to rise from its grave. He got a chisel and began, with fury, to carve out the table. Cut, cut, cut. Mother and I stared and stared, anxious not to miss the sparkling object amid the curled shavings.

"Don't go so fast!" mother shouted.

He slowed down. I ran over to the rack, got another chisel and wanted to join in, but his harsh voice stopped me.

"Put it back!"

I did.

He'd exhausted himself and still no diamond.

"How much – how much is it worth?" mother's voice was barely more than a whisper. Siggy didn't reply. He was exhausted: his head was on the bench, his breathing came in big gasps, his back heaved. Mother went over, bent down and kissed his cheek, and tears came into his eyes. I couldn't stand a man crying and turned away. I'd have given the earth for that diamond to appear, and then, as if by some malignant fate, the Nazi gangs came again and so did the cursed Horst Wessel song. We all listened with shivers running down our spines at the brutal but haunting melody.

"THERE it is!!" I'd spotted it – dulled and covered by tiny bits of sawdust, it lay, an innocent symbol of a boy's revenge, of the devil in the soul.

Note 1

The Austrian Nazis were very active before the Anschluss (annexation of Austria to Germany in March 1938). They were led by Seyss-Inquart and did very much as they wished. The Austrian police were reluctant to deal with them and they (the Nazis) terrified the Jews.

'Nothing to smile about'
Mother's family (The Grünbergs) taken while under Nazi occupation

Top left: Uncle Henry (inventor of the only all-Austrian bicycle). Next to him, his wife, Irma. Top right: Uncle Leo - merchant banker, instrumental in developing Wiener Neustadt as an industrial centre. Front left: Uncle Siggy - craftsman jeweller; myself; mother; her sister, Aunt Annie; and cousin Heinz, now living in Southport.

Part 2

THE ANSCHLUSS

Chapter 4

The Nazis arrive

The university square was large – the surrounding buildings were grand, black and gothic. The tram lines criss-crossed each other in coils. I loved these trams – always in pairs, a dirty red, with the impassive driver swivelling his brass lever while his luckier conductor at least had people to talk to.

As the students charged all over the place, there wasn't exactly chaos but a kind of heightened activity, a fever of movement. They jumped on the trams, shouted directions to each other all wearing the coloured caps of their faculties – green, red, blue – badges of pride in their battle with the dark green police who had arrived in special vans open at both sides for jumping on and off quickly.

Mother sat looking straight ahead of her: "Don't look – just mind your own business," she commanded. But how could I? There was too much going on, too much excitement. Some students jumped on our tram, the conductor (wanting no trouble) ignored them while continuing to clip our tickets. Soon they jumped off and raced toward their fellows who were in a fracas with other students and police.

All I knew was that there were two sides fighting each other, and, being a normal boy, I felt the blood of battle rise within me. But whose side should I support? It was all confusion.

* * * * *

The market place was at the end of our street – the place a 'respectable' type like me wasn't supposed to visit. It was a square full of delight, full of colour, of squashed vegetables on the ground, of loud types shouting their wares and small black boards with the prices written in white chalk.

At the end of the square was a cluster of people with a large red-white-red Austrian flag as background. One man shouted down a loud hailer, others walked soberly round distributing leaflets – even I was given one. But I sensed the boredom. An election soon? What *is* an election? I sensed it was a 'good' thing. I liked the flag – it gave me a patriotic thrill – it was *my* flag and I heard a loud hailer shout: "We're Austrians, not Germans. Down with Seyss-Inquart!" (Nazi leader) but before a single vote was due to be cast on the 14th, Hitler's troops marched into Austria on the 13th March, 1938. Not a hand was raised against them, not a drop of blood was spilt, flowers were thrown under their feet. The Austrians sensed greatness again. After the First World War they had been humiliated – they had lost an Empire, they had been reduced to a small country of little significance. Now they would join the Third Reich and power would be theirs again.

Meanwhile in Juden Gasse (Jew Street), a few miles away, we skulked behind closed shutters too frightened even to go into the street. Through the tiny hole I'd cut into the window shutter with my penknife, we could see into the street – it was empty, it was eerie. Where was Mrs Klapholz, where were the Abram children, where was my grand-dad sitting, ever dozing, on his little stool in front of his second-hand clothes shop, a shop which never seemed to sell anything; where, above all, were the energetic Shapiros, the owners of the above-average clothes store that, we sensed, would soon be too good for us. We, the ghetto people, the little people, we seemed to have disappeared.

The bakelite radio on the kitchen table was our only contact with the outside world. It crackled depressing news: Chancellor Schuchnigg's old, weary voice pleaded: 'Avoid bloodshed,' 'Keep order,' 'Obey authority'. But my simple young mind said: 'Coward – you can always fight!!'

It was on the second day that I heard the eeriest of sounds. It was like a wail – it rose and subsided with the wind: one moment it was terrifyingly near, then it receded into a whisper. No, it was no wail, it was a human mass cheering themselves hoarse – the Viennese were openly, unashamedly welcoming their Saviour. Mother sat tight-lipped: "Must be a million, must be a million," she muttered.

Later we learnt it was nearer two million who had, overnight, become besotted by the Führer, who would follow him wherever he led – to glory or damnation.

But still we hadn't seen a German. Where were the dreaded SS, where were the anti-Semitic mobs, the looters, the louts, and so on?

True, at the end of our street we heard lorries trundling past – army lorries, we presumed, bringing the might of the Nazis to occupy us. Thank goodness, they left our cobbled, old-fashioned street alone. We were just congratulating ourselves on our luck when one lorry did *not* go past. With infinite slowness it turned into the street, it lumbered past number 1, then past our place, number 3, further it went up the street, like some invading beast, and stopped outside the Shapiros. A couple of soldiers, looking very much like our Austrian army – same helmets, same rumpled grey uniforms – jumped down, and, shouting into the stillness, pointed to the Shapiro shop. They went over. It was locked and bolted. They rattled the big lock, then turning across the street, and, standing in the middle of the road, shouted up: "Shapiro – Jew – come out!" No answer – just the blankness of brown shutters. "Throw down your keys." Yet more silence. Mum muttered to herself: "Give them the keys – it's only clothes!" We heard a high-pitched woman's voice from inside the Shapiros. "It's Shabbat – a holy day. We don't touch keys on holy days!" This simply stimulated them. They unslung their rifles from round their shoulders, pointed them upwards: "Throw down your keys!" They clicked their bolts.

"Oh, my God!" muttered mum, "Shapiro don't be stupid!" I couldn't quite believe it – such things don't happen. And then, the great front door of the Shapiro's place opened and a woman's hand was seen holding out the keys. A soldier grabbed not only the keys but the arm as well and she was dragged across the street, and, with some difficulty, the other soldier opened the lock and the two doors swung back. Then, told by a warning finger to stay where she was, they began, without hurry, to empty the shop and throw the clothes – and fine clothes they were – into the lorry.

Mrs Shapiro stood, her hand to her mouth, as if in a dream. I thought she might faint. I wondered if she'd scream, or have the shakes; but no, for quite a while, as the two soldiers emptied her shop, she simply stood. Perhaps her fortitude affected them, I don't know, but while pillaging the shop they said nothing. And when the shop lay dark and empty, they threw the keys into the road, got into the lorry and drove off.

After they'd gone, she still stood there, until her husband, considerably older, tottered across to her and gently led her home. Then she remembered the keys and went back, stooped to pick them up. The keys were safe! A shopkeeper's instinct had prompted her to hold on to them.

The looting of the Shapiro shop made me feel glad that we were poor. We had nothing worth taking, nothing they could loot, so perhaps we would go unnoticed. Our family name was not known, surely they will leave us alone. Even in those early days, self-preservation was uppermost. We were thinking: 'Thank heaven it's the Shapiro shop and not us', and the even worse thought: 'They're rich enough to bounce back again.'

This open looting of a shop became a turning point – for this was no longer rumour but fact: we had seen with our own eyes ruthless, anti-Semitic power. And there was no redress, no running to authority to complain. No, we were helpless, and, at every house and every street corner this fact was made plain to us, for Vienna had become dressed up with gigantic Nazi flags and wherever one looked there were uniforms.

Mother tried to turn her head away, tried not to look, but I gawped, for, Shapiro or not, the glamour of Nazism got to me.

I became fascinated by the gradations of power. The Agricultural Corps were at the bottom – mere labourers dressed up in brown militarism, then came the army, rumpled in their functional grey. The police underwent a transformation from the rather squashed appearance of the apologetic Austrian police to a very dignified light green with splendid domed helmets. But, towering above the rest, resplendent in their superiority, were the SA and the SS. Even here grades were important: the SA – mustard brown, jack-booted, with swastika armbands, emitted an overpowering arrogance, but even they were one down from the SS. These god-like beings hardly bothered with mere Jewish boys or women. Their uniforms were the work of genius: black and silver with a skull and crossbones emblem.

They were so superior their eyes slid across us for we were hardly worth looking at.

Of course the SS had pride of place in my secret book. This work of betrayal was kept under my bed. There, in detailed drawings, I recorded all uniforms and insignia, finishing with the Hitler Youth. I knew, had circumstances been different, I might have been one of them. So confused was my mind, so schizoid my attitude, that one minute I loathed the invader, I abhorred and was frightened by what had happened to the Shapiros, yet simultaneously, I could not rid myself of the magnetism the victorious have for a youngster.

But when the atrocities started there was no room for hesitation. When Jewish boys and girls were hounded down the street beside the Danube, when shops had 'Jude' daubed on them, when the police stood idly by while youths beat up a bearded Jew, then compromise was out. This was no longer the Austria which held my patriotism. I had been a fervent patriot. I had sung the national anthem with vigour, I had revered the flag, I had supported the football team and gone to a state school. But no longer did this country hold my allegiance. Instead I seethed at our humiliation, I wanted badly to hit back. But how wild are a boy's aspirations, how powerless his limbs!

We could do nothing. There was no redress to law. There was nowhere we could turn. They could do with us what they wanted.

I was lucky enough to be protected form the worst excesses, but two incidents stood out. I remember the rush of feet, and tearing past me, with black hair streaming, was a Jewish girl being chased by Hitler Youths. There was unforgettable terror on her face. Another vision was of a small crowd staring down at something in their midst. And there, on the floor, were the black-robed, bearded rabbis – our leaders – scrubbing the pavement with toothbrushes. Two immaculate SS men strutted among them. A mother (heaven help her) lifted up her son so he could get a better view, a lout laughed, another aimed a kick. I looked hard at the crowd of Austrians, not one of them showed disgust, not one of them turned away.

By this time most of us realised that our only hope was escape. But where to? Possibilities flashed before me – all empty names except England – the most powerful country in the world and the only one I felt would stand up to the Nazis.

We were to try a great many countries. Not one of them would open its frontiers and welcome us in. They had their own troubles in this time of world recession, and Jews were not the most popular of people. Work permits had to be obtained and visas asked for, and most countries simply refused entry. Nor did the Germans help. Yes, they wanted the 'Jewish Question' resolved, but they would make it as difficult as possible. They would squeeze every drop of perverted pleasure out of the process.

Picture of Jews forced to scrub pavements by Nazis in Vienna. Note expressions of onlookers. (By courtesy of the BBC, Hulton-Getty Library)

Chapter 5

The Long Wait

Now it was queuing time outside Vienna's main synagogue. To humiliate us the Nazis appropriated all famous Jewish buildings and used them as part of their bureaucratic machine. The main synagogue was an obvious target, as was the Rothschild Palace. So, if you needed a vital document to leave Vienna, you had to get it from a place which demonstrated your helplessness and humiliation.

So the queues formed – queues that lasted several days and nights, queues which, paradoxically, revived my spirits, for, at least, we were doing something, at least there was hope that here we'd get the paper which would allow us to leave and look for a country that would take us in.

As I joined the queue a few adults smiled at me; one even said: "You can borrow my stool."

After some time of shyness, we thawed and a few began to show off: "I've got a cousin in Shanghai." "The States have said 'Yes' – all we need is for the Germans to give us this permit." "We're only doing this in case things get worse – as an insurance."

Slowly the queue moved forward – we counted how many were in front of us – and God help anyone who tried to push in! The night was cold and gradually my eyes closed, so, long after my normal bedtime, I surrendered to a disturbed, uncomfortable sleep.

I woke up through the cold and looked round: 'Where was mum?' Panic! I tugged at a man's sleeve: "My mum – ?" "Don't worry, she's gone home to the toilet. I'll look after you." I got a smile; I also sensed a feeling of communion. Up to now, fear had driven us to compete with each other, it caused rifts, it prompts you to shut yourself up with your nearest and dearest, but there, an unknown man was looking after me. Queues are social levellers, they create their own loyalties. Now I didn't mind queues – I even liked them. And then came an incident that completely threw me.

It happened later that morning as the sun had thawed out our limbs and mum had long ago returned. There were only three people in front of us. At the synagogue's entrance an SS man was regulating the flow. He let the three in and stopped mum and me, and then he stared down at me, he paused, and, with the very faintest of smiles, he let mum and me through. I could scarcely believe it. So awesome, so high and mighty – the SS – such terrifying gods – and yet this simple act of kindness! But this momentary impulse was instantly wiped out by the sight of the inside of the synagogue.

Here 'religion' had been eradicated: the Ark had gone, so had the whole bima[2], the eternal light had been torn from the ceiling, the carpets had been stolen, leaving edge marks as a reminder; there were nasty burn marks on the walls; every now and then, the pews had been hacked down, and, in their stead, were trestle tables round which a few military functionaries worked. They bullied their way through the cringing Jews who daren't do anything but mumble a servile 'yes' or 'no' in answer to queries. The Jews watched the eyes of the functionaries to see if the 'yes' of salvation was to be stamped on their paper.

Our man showed only the top of his shiny, brown head. He asked mum questions without looking up; shy and frightened, she mumbled answers. She grasped my hand for comfort, she held it so tight it hurt. Suddenly the man looked up and barked a question at her. I couldn't fathom it but heard the words 'Das Kind' – that meant me. So I was the focus of all this, perhaps I would be the reason for not getting the paper. Mum could barely answer. The man shouted: "Speak up!" Something revolted in her at this bullying and she all but shouted back: "He's coming with me!"

Surprisingly, the man became more reasonable – so standing up to bullying *had* worked. I felt proud of mum.

Of course I was to go with her – there was no doubt about it. Nothing, but nothing would split us up! I was as sure of this as anything in the world.

I watched the man stamp the document and saw him hand it over. With ill-disguised joy we almost ran out of the synagogue. Outside, in the sunlight, we looked at the precious piece of paper. My mum's face fell. All it was was permission to seek permission to leave the glories of the Third Reich. They'd simply placed another hurdle in our way, made the path to freedom seem even further away.

Note 2

A bima is a raised platform in a synagogue on which many ceremonies are carried out.

Chapter 6

A Horror

Around this time we heard the dreadful news of Uncle Siggy's suicide. Everyone tried hard to keep it from me, but it caused too general distress for me to be unaware of it; mother, especially, seemed unable to get over it. This poor man, who had been dogged by misfortune since childhood, who had scrambled his way through life while creating beautiful objects, who was kindness and generosity itself – simply faced facts and cheated the Nazis of a victim. There was no hope for him – he was a cripple and he was a Jew – on both counts he would sooner or later disappear into a camp and suffer unimaginable horrors. Perhaps he chose the best way, but at the time we couldn't see it like that.

He had but one memorial – the ring I had watched him make for that 'attractive lady'. At last I knew who she was; and my mother wore it until she died in 1989.

Chapter 7

Robert

With my back against the green school railings, I watched, with envy, the football toughies in all their vigour and excitement. A small boy, minute among those giants, was weaving in and out, the ball glued to his feet, leaving them bewildered in their clumsiness. Suddenly, to my surprise, he left the game, came over to me and said: "You go home through Kärtnerstrasse, don't you?" I nodded. "Right, we'll go together," and with that he returned to the game. Not, I noted, '*Shall* we go home together?' but we *will* go home together, and that was that. I was much bigger than him, but from the word go he was the leader of our 'gang of two' and I the follower. It was automatic and I was quite content in my role for there was a tremendous exuberance about Robert – he seemed more alive than others, his imagination more active, and, on the way home he'd scour Vienna's twisty streets for signs of interest – and certainly there was plenty about, for in mid-summer 1938 the place was dressed up in the red, white and black of huge waving swastika flags and wherever one looked there were SS men or green-dressed policemen with their strange tub-like hats, and, of course, there were the officers – the strutting commanders of everything and everyone – the Lords of Creation. No one got in their way, everyone stared in open admiration, and Robert was fascinated by them.

"There's a new one!" he shouted excitedly, pointing towards a strange, chocolate-coloured uniform with a long peaked cap. "Do you know what that one is?" I pretended I didn't.

"Agricultural Corps," he said, knowingly.

"What on earth do *they* want a uniform for?" I asked.

"Everyone wants a uniform. *I* want a uniform, *you* want a uniform ..."

"No!" I blurted out.

"What do you mean 'no'?" he'd stopped, astonished, so rare was a contradiction from me. I said: "We Jews don't want uniforms – uniforms are the enemy."

It was a huge gamble considering how important Robert had become to me, for I couldn't be 100% certain he *was* a Jew. Now he put his face close to mine and jabbed his finger into my shoulder: "That's our trouble – we're too timid. *We* should get dressed up, we should organise." And then, as if embarrassed by such seriousness, he jumped on to a wall, arms stretched out, bird-like, and ran along it fast. I followed, arms also outstretched and didn't care if I fell off, for all I could think of was that he was one of us, and I was as happy as a bird.

But soon Robert's excitability and couldn't-care-less attitude disturbed me for he began to follow SS men. I sensed he did this as a test of his own courage. He followed them quite closely, with me in tow, and if the SS man happened to turn round, Robert would be seen gazing innocently into the distance or looking into a shop window. "Detectives do that," he confided, "I've seen it on the films."

"What if they catch us?" I asked anxiously.

"Ah!" he said mysteriously.

"What do you mean 'ah'?"

He grinned, "They'd torture us."

"Don't be daft!"

"Well," he looked thoughtful, "there *is* torture in Vienna." Suddenly the whole idea gripped him: "What do you know of torture? Come on, tell me." I searched my memory of history books: "The drip, drip on the forehead..?" I volunteered.

"That's Chinese and old-fashioned."

"Come on, I'll show you!" And he was off, racing down the street with me after him. Soon we came to a very high grey wall. He stopped. "Behind here," he rapped the wall with his knuckle, "screams are heard every night." I could almost 'see' the men and their instruments behind the wall, and, suddenly, the whole idea of Nazis, of their uniforms, their flags, became real and fearsome. It was no longer a child's game but a hideous fact that might touch me and my family. I'd already heard of people disappearing into 'camps'. What if Uncle Leo, Aunt Marie, or, heaven forbid, mum didn't turn up one day for supper?

Robert was now looking at me with a smile on his face.

"How long would you hold out," he asked, "if they tortured you?"

We stared at each other.

"Not long," I admitted (I was a realist).

"Too much for you, is it?"

I nodded, prepared for his contempt, but instead he began to walk away from the wall. "Yes," he said, thoughtfully nodding his head, "It's your imagination that's the problem – But I'll tell you one thing – " he stopped and looked squarely at me.

"They'd never break me."

* * * * *

Suddenly it was announced that all Jewish children were to be put into separate schools. Mum was pleased: "At least you'll be with kids of your own kind," she said, and, as long as Robert came with me I didn't care. Thank goodness we soon discovered that Robert and I were to go to the same school.

The place wasn't too bad: a tall, three-storey building, so empty of everything but the bare essentials that it echoed constantly to children's noise. Coming downstairs for break was like a rumbling thunderstorm. It was obviously not meant to be permanent – a point reinforced by round-shouldered, defeated-looking teachers who showed little interest in teaching. We could do more or less as we liked, and what we discussed endlessly was: "Where are you off to?" meaning, which country would let you in during the wild rush to leave Nazi Vienna. Would it be France, England, the States? – anywhere in the wide world where it was 'safe'. Everyone swanked: "My dad's got a factory in Shanghai," "We've got relatives in Peru". Robert and I turned our backs on this, for my fear wasn't of not getting out, but of having to leave him, and, when one day mum came home brandishing a piece of paper: "Look, we've got a visa to England; I've got a job as a domestic servant with the Misses Fisher in Bournemouth!" I simply couldn't join in her celebrations.

"What's the matter, long face?" she asked, puzzled, "Aren't you happy?"

"Where's Robert going?" I asked.

"How should *I* know. For heaven's sake – look!" and she pushed the piece of paper under my nose. "This could save our lives!"

It took a lot of doing to get myself to ask Robert the crucial question: "Where are *you* going?" He glanced up at me, his mind plainly elsewhere:

"Not sure – Switzerland, I think."

My heart sank: "Not England?"

"No," but he seemed barely interested. Instead he said: "Look at this!" and he thrust in front of me very detailed drawings he'd made of SS insignia, from the lowest grade to Herr General. "Aren't they terrific?" In the past I'd made very similar drawings which I now regarded with shame, they seemed to me pure treachery.

He went on proudly: "I can tell you every SS rank, and the SA as well – haven't got all the army yet..."

"WHAT FOR?" I burst out in frustration.

He was taken aback.

"What do you mean?" he asked.

"Why are you doing this? They're the enemy for God's sake!"

"Exactly!" Now he became enthusiastic: "Know your enemy – first rule of war!"

"What war?"

"What do you mean 'what war'?"

"Just what I said – what war?"

"Between us and them, of course – the Jews and Nazis!" It was perfectly obvious to him. Frankly, I thought he was a bit unhinged – us, a powerless lot of civilians against the might of – it was incredible! He was watching me closely: "You don't believe it, do you – that we'll ever fight?" I shook my head. Then he lost control and shouted:

"That's our trouble – we won't fight – just let them roll all over us!"

"How can we?"

"You *can* always fight!" And he clenched his small fists and stared away from me. Surely, I thought, he doesn't believe that himself – but with Robert I was never sure. And, suddenly, I saw how very different we were. He, the fighter, and I the realist who refused to follow wild fantasy and was, perhaps, just a bit afraid. Perhaps these differences would affect our friendship – become an awkward area of conflict – but, surely, I argued with myself, not a complete break – I simply wouldn't entertain such an idea.

* * * * *

"Back! Back!" shouted the little bearded teacher, holding out his arms in an effort to stop a stream of boys. Some got past him and ran towards the huge front door. "Come back here!" he shouted hysterically, "Don't turn that key!" The boys halted, walked slowly back, demanding to know what was going on. "Never mind. Back to your classes. Go on – *upstairs*!" He was all but screaming. Speculating, bewildered, we did as we were told, and, on returning to our classroom, saw a group of boys by the window, staring at something down below. We joined them and saw, some distance from the school, a mass of Hitler Youths with their immaculate white shirts, short black corduroy trousers and small gleaming knives. Behind them was a group of civilians, simply watching. The Hitler Youths were trying to organise themselves – a tall, blond boy gesticulating orders. It soon became obvious they were making a ring round the school – each boy about three metres from the next, hands behind his back, daring us to come out. There was a policeman there, but he was right at the back, plainly showing it had nothing to do with him. The crowd was increasing, people talking, gesticulating, pointing. We looked round for our teachers – where *were* they? Why weren't they *here*? A sense of helplessness spread among us – no one knew what to do. I looked round for Robert, who, being so small, had jumped on to a desk to look over our heads at the scene below, but he was lost in thought – unapproachable. Then naked fear took over – would they attack, throw stones, try and break down the door? Afraid to show my fear, I walked away to be alone, but the window soon drew me back, and as I turned round, I saw the desk Robert had been standing on – empty. Where on earth – ? Had he gone to the toilet? I went outside to look for him – no sign of him, and then I happened to look down into the hall and there he was – fully dressed to go home, satchel bouncing on his bottom – walking casually across the marble floor as though nothing had happened. His actions implied: 'It was going home time, so I'm going home'. He had a job with the old-fashioned door key – but managed it. A shaft of sunlight came in as he opened the large door, then darkness again as it closed behind him. I raced back to the classroom window. Where was he – ? No sign of him. I realised, he must be right underneath us. And then I saw the top of his brown head and the swinging satchel appear below us. He was walking casually across the empty space towards the ring of boys. They and the crowd were now still, all looking at the tiny figure moving, unconcerned, towards them. What would happen when he reached the ring? Would they block his path; push him back, even beat him up? But everyone seemed mesmerised – it was almost like a dream with him sleep-walking towards the tall boys. He ambled on and was now very near two boys, but his pace didn't change. As if going for a stroll, he simply walked towards the gap between them. The boys looked at each other, hesitated, and then Robert was through, weaving his way through the crowd. No one stopped him, some even gave way, and they all swivelled round to stare at him, and then he was lost to sight.

We didn't talk, we didn't cheer, we simply looked at each other in astonishment. We saw the crowd eagerly talk among themselves, and then, the show over, one or two drifted away, and then some more. The Hitler Youths were arguing among themselves and the blond boy was pointing towards the school, but then some of *them* began to drift. Soon only a few were left and then this small group walked disconsolately away. The square was empty now except for the lone policeman who stood staring into the distance.

Chapter 8

The Chase

Robert's bravery made me feel a little freer, a little less frightened; of the Nazis. It was not a transformation by any means, but a lessening of tension so that the uniforms stalking our streets were no longer completely dominant. Occasionally I'd even be a little cheeky and it was this that nearly led to disaster.

It was due to mother's habit of referring everything to God. If the sun shone then God was pleased with mankind and smiled upon us, but if it hailed and thundered then we'd committed some terrible misdeed.

So, one day, when we were caught in one of Vienna's violent rain-storms, I shouted to mother above the rain's noise:

"God's angry with us!"

"What?"

"I said God's angry with us!"

And then, as the rain died down, I added:

"He's angry because the Nazis are here."

What I hadn't noticed were the footsteps quite close behind us – not civilian footsteps, but the now familiar sound of jackboots. Because the rain had died down, my voice sounded very loud.

Mother went pale, she grabbed my hand and pulled me behind her, not running but walking very fast.

The jackboots followed and neither of us dared turn round.

Mother pulled me round the next corner and, for a second, there was no sound of jackboots, but then they came again and they were very close.

Despite mother's panting, she hissed angrily:

"Why did you say that – why now – in the street?"

"But the rain was so loud, I never thought anyone would hear!"

"You never think, do you!"

"Where are we going?"

"Not home, that's for certain – he'll know where we live!" And she pulled me even harder.

"But where?"

It was obvious she didn't know. She turned one corner after another at random, but the boots were still behind us. It was plain the man was toying with us – or else he'd have arrested us there and then. We got so confused that, with the twists and turns of streets, we suddenly found ourselves where we didn't want to be – in the market square very near our street. But mother was delighted: "Good," she said, "now we can lose him among the stalls!" And she pulled me here and there, almost pulling my hand off, so it seemed impossible for anyone to keep up with us. Exhausted, she stopped, and leant against a wall, panting. I felt giddy. Then mother looked back and went even paler: "SS," she mumbled, and, grabbing me, she turned blindly into our street. I followed as best I could, almost stumbling on the cobbles. Into our house she ran, through the great doorway, up the stairs, fumbled for her keys, and, ushering me in, she banged the door shut.

We couldn't speak, we were panting so hard and I saw her chest heave up and down. I recovered before she did and glanced towards the window, and 'Heaven help us' the shutters were open! I rushed towards them when, behind me, mother's voice screamed: "Leave them open or he'll know which floor we're on!" Too late! The instinct to hide, made me bang the shutters to.

"You fool!" she yelled, "now he'll come up!"

I rushed towards the hole in the shutters I'd made with my penknife; looked right, looked left. Thank heaven there was no sign of him – in fact, the street was eerily empty.

I was just about to let mum know we were safe when I saw him. He was standing directly opposite us in the shadow of a doorway and looking straight up at us. He knew where we were!

In a leisurely fashion he fumbled in his top pocket. Out came a notebook. He leant forward to peer at the number of our house and began making notes – all very slowly and deliberately. For a moment I thought I wouldn't tell mother – I would lie. But that wasn't my way. I turned round and looked at her. She looked back.

"Well?"

I nodded, "He's there."

She brushed me aside to peer for herself through the hole; she stood there for quite a while and then said in a whisper: "Now he knows where we are." And then she broke down. It was sudden, it was horrible. She put her head down on the table and sobbed and sobbed as if her soul was breaking.

I've never felt more helpless, more lost. I went back to the hole expecting him to be there, but, to my joy and surprise, he'd gone – no sign of him.

I turned back to look at mum and said, very quietly: "He's gone, we're safe."

Hardly daring to believe me, she looked appealingly at me. I nodded, "Really – he's gone." She didn't bother to check, she got up, went towards the kitchen and shut me out.

We heard nothing more of this. No doubt, in some file, we were marked down, but, for the time being, we'd survived.

Chapter 9

Kristallnacht

Kristallnacht finally extinguished all hope that any Jew of any description – rich, poor, old, young, secular or fromm – could live a reasonable life in Nazi Austria. On this evening of 9-10th November, 1938, every adult male Jew who the Nazis could lay their hands on was arrested and carted off into the mysterious dark. Some came back, some were never seen again. Jewish Vienna was virtually eliminated, synagogues erased, shops smashed. The name 'Night of Tinkling Glass' was born.

But for me Kristallnacht was a private affair. Up to now mum had protected me, sheltered me and kept normality going. But on that night we were terrified. We turned off the light and skulked in our flat. Let there be no sign, no chink of light. We heard rampaging jackboots, much shouting, the hysterical screams of a woman whose husband was grabbed and the terminal snap of car doors shutting on their victims. 'What of dad?' our thoughts were as one, but nothing was said, and, Kristallnacht or not, I fell asleep, head on the table, recalling nothing other than a pillow placed gently under my head.

Next day, I don't know how, a message reached us and mum grabbed me: "Your coat and shoes – come on!" She didn't even wait for me to get these on before she was half way down the street and running towards the 'other place'. I couldn't make it out – surely that was forbidden territory for her. What *had* happened? A constriction in my stomach told me the world had turned upside down, and there she now was at the brown front door of dad's flat, and she went inside as though she lived there, and there, on the chequered stone floor and in front of the lift, was Rosa – but not *my* Rosa – self-confident, almost arrogant – no, a shrunken Rosa – crying, eyes red, and she and mum looked at each other for a moment and then crashed into each other's arms. I watched amazed – all the rules broken, the antipathy which I'd expected shelved as they hugged and comforted each other. Rosa just mumbled: "He's safe," and mum burst into tears and the women tacitly acknowledged a love linked by invisible threads to dad.

Mum remembered I was there, held out her hand and I took it. "He's safe, he's safe!" she exclaimed, and I was not to know this was only a reprieve, a momentary lapse, in a saga in which the accident of history permitted only one bond to remain unbroken – that of mum and myself – the rest was swallowed up.

Meanwhile dad was upstairs in Rosa's flat trying to get his shattered nerves together. For a few days he wouldn't talk of his ordeal. Then he asked Rosa, mum and myself to listen to him: "They sealed off the streets and grabbed every adult Jewish man. No explanation as to where we were going or why we were arrested. 'March' was the order and march we did. We were taken to the barracks and lined up – some prayed, some thought it was the end.

"We were being sorted out – but for what – for work? We didn't know and they weren't going to tell us for every second of ignorance increased our anxiety. At the end of a long line of men we saw an ordinary sergeant, not even an officer. He was sitting, feet up, at a desk. As you came before him, he looked at you, he held your life in his eye for a second, then he spoke harshly: "*You* Dachau," "*You* go home," "*You* too weak," "Send him back to the end of the line," (the cruellest touch), and so on." Dad stopped, and mum, who had drunk in every word, leant forward and asked: "What happened to you?" Dad replied: "I was lucky," and he burst into tears.

The aftermath of Kristallnacht was 44 synagogues desecrated, hundreds of Jewish shops destroyed, and Vienna covered in glass. Several thousand men from District 1 had disappeared and the concentration camp at Dachau was now a word of awe. But thereafter no Jew thought of anything else but escape.

But where to? Anywhere and everywhere. It didn't matter. Some of the most bizarre names came up – Bolivia, Burma, Venezuela – names known to me only from postage stamps. Göring warned us that to be a refugee was grim, but, we thought, it was better than being dead.

Chapter 10

Goodbye Vienna

For us, it was always England. To get there you had to have a permit to show you had a job waiting. Fair enough, for the country had millions of unemployed. How mother managed to get a work permit giving her a job as a domestic servant with the Misses Fisher of Bournemouth I shall never know. Agencies helped, Quakers helped, kind people helped. Some famous, the Attenboroughs, for instance, employed several refugees as servants simply to get them out of Germany or Austria.

But all that was still in the future, still part of the excitement as well as the uncertainty. England seemed a million miles away. We had learnt not to take anything for granted.

When, finally, we had surmounted every hurdle the Nazis put in front of us; when we were loaded with official-looking documents and had gathered every penny we could, even then there were several heart-stopping moments on the way.

On the Westbahnhof we were waiting for dad beside the train to Ostend. This was to be our final goodbye. Mum couldn't stop still, she crumpled her handkerchief, her eyes were glued to the barrier, and then: "There he is!" she yelled and rushed towards him and embraced him so fiercely I thought she'd never let go. I saw that, divorce or not, she still thought of him as her husband, that, in a profound sense, he was hers. How I wished I was part of that embrace! That he'd have come to me, towsled my hair, kissed me, that he'd have said something that would have brought his voice back to me. But then the train started to move and mum had to let go, grab my hand, and we were both bundled into the train. My last sight of dad was of a figure running by the side of the train waving into the air, and I was left with the hope that at least some of this was for me.

All the way through Austria, through Salzkammergut, through Bavaria, the Rhineland, through some of the most touristy countryside in Europe, we went with not a moment's thought for the scenery, for we were haunted by fear, knowing we could *still* be stopped, our papers examined, errors found by arrogant, jumped-up officials enjoying their power. Every time the train jerked to a halt we tried to shrink into invisibility. We never glanced out of the carriage and avoided everyone's eyes. Nor did we speak much to each other. Yes, we were all escapees. But you never know, someone might betray us. The habit of caution, of silence, of fear was by now ingrained into every muscle and nerve.

Yet, despite this constant vigil and caution, I was doggedly hopeful. England lay ahead of us! And in my mind even if Europe went dark there would be one beacon of light – I was certain of that, and always believed there was a destiny for me in that country. I do not know where such optimism had its roots. Perhaps in three thousand years of survival.

At long last, after two days and a night, we came to Aachen – the last bit of Germany, the last place where strutting jackboots could instil fear. We saw one SS man – the final symbol of a hated regime.

Then the train slowly, all too slowly, moved forward towards Belgium. I tried to imagine where the border was. Where was the exact line where we would be free? And then, to everyone's relief, the carriage door crashed open, and large, magnificently over-dressed Belgian policemen demanded our papers. These officials were straight out of operetta and we almost expected them to burst into song. But a uniform was still a uniform and for a second I felt anxiety. And then they wished us 'Gutentag' and laughed. Joyously, we handed over our papers, they looked at them perfunctorily, and, as soon as they were gone, we began to laugh and joke, anxious to become more acquainted with our equally fortunate neighbours. Freedom at last – and in its most tangible form – an absence of fear!

But mother and I knew there was one more hurdle to overcome and it could have undone all we'd achieved so far.

In Dover the Customs Officer looked bored as he took passports, visas, documents mechanically. He turned the pages while we stared at him anxiously for we knew there was a flaw. He glanced at the two of us. That was the point, there were two of us and the passport showed one. Mother was on there, I was not. He was about to let it go when he stopped. he looked again. Then he said awkwardly: "The child, das Kind?" Mother bit her lip. She said stubbornly: "I'm not sending him back. How can I?" The man looked at her – the hiatus lasted a second. Not for an instance did I doubt mum – she simply wouldn't abandon me. I felt utterly secure.

The man stamped the passport and waved us on. Because of the generosity of an English Customs Officer I entered this country.

Part 3

ENGLAND, OH ENGLAND

Chapter 11

A Nazi in Hampstead

In England there was no way mother and I could stay together. She had to make her way to Bournemouth to the Misses Fisher as a servant and nothing in her contract allowed her to bring children. Yet my trust in her was absolute – we were indissoluble – she would always be there – she was the one certainty in an uncertain world. But now we had to part. Yet wasn't this England, the land of magic, the land of glory and freedom, so instead of anxiety, I faced the future with confidence, and, when I was told that for a time, just for a *very* short time, I would be living with Dr and Mrs Baum in Belsize Park, I wasn't in the least disturbed. In fact, I was excited: would anyone speak German (I knew no English); what was an English school like; and how long would these strange words bombard me? The oddest words seemed to stick in my imagination; 'wee' was one of the first, then came 'Kit-Kat' and 'Aero'. But, although Dr Baum and I sat down to our breakfast every morning, yet I can hardly remember any 'breakfast' words. What I do recall was the ultra-white tablecloth, starched until it cracked, a shiny toast-rack with neat triangular toasts and glistening marmalade in a cut-glass dish – all in front of the Times which hid from me the slightly awe-inspiring Dr Baum.

He was my umbilical cord to Hampstead and beyond – he bridged German and English and told me what I must and must not do: "You say 'please' and 'thank-you'. You read 25 lines every night and list new words; and for fun – here you are!" In a shower of coloured rain he spilt several hundred stamps on to the table. It was sheer joy to put them into my green 6 penny Woolworth album – each lovingly licked by a hinge. They were my window on a bizarre world: dolphins on huge triangular stamps, flying goalkeepers over the word Helvetia, and, disappointingly, dull English stamps with a disembodied king's head.

Why not a more majestic stamp for this Imperial island? Why not a trumpeting of glory by the world's greatest Imperial power? And so, by way of these bits of paper, I learnt of English reticence, of under-statement, of the no-need-to-shout philosophy that puzzled and bemused this temperamental child who had just come from a steel-clasped Vienna where the death-squads stalked.

But English calm can be unnerving: the ram-rod straight, dark-haired maid with the taut lines of nerves on her face and flickers of hate in her eyes never said a word. But at tea, while cutting my Swiss roll, I sensed her disgust at having to serve this stranger in *her* lush flat. And what of Mrs Baum, that quiet blond ghost flickering from room to room whose dressing-gown kept coming undone to expose knobbly white knees? Why no word from her? Why no loving, comforting breasts that cuddled and consoled? Why that cool draught of reticence that puzzled and kept me out? Even the dog said nothing. Large and conceited in his magnificence, he had adopted from his English master and mistress an English reserve.

Dr Baum's walk with me was a daily ceremony. He had a Pickwickian stomach and grey immaculate gloves; he carried a brass-studded dog lead in one hand and a neatly folded carrier-bag (Dickens & Jones) in the other. He was always dressed either in black or brown, and walked with an air of enjoyment, always finishing with a packet of hand-picked chocolates for the blond ghost who greeted him with a faint smile and what passed for a kiss (a reserved peck). I watched this reticence with wonder – my mother, on father's home-coming, would either shriek foul-mouthed accusations of betrayal at him or crash into his arms with a sexuality even I found thrilling. What varieties of human types the globe contained!

But leave me, leave me to my lovely stamps, and put off that dreaded word 'school' which kept coming up, and, with it, the words 'Jenny and Arthur'. I'd watch these two balancing on walls opposite. I'd see them swirl with out-stretched arms – playing aeroplanes; I'd see them swing round the green Victorian lamp-post at the corner of the road and then disappear towards St. Paul's Junior. Friends or enemies? There was no way of knowing ... yet.

The leather-stiff, shiny brown satchel was round my chest. Inside were two neat exercise-books, two pencils, one rubber and a white ruler. And then I was pushed into the big world of Belsize Rd., where Jenny and Arthur watched the newcomer with wide eyes. They had instructions to take me to school. We managed to walk in utter silence (no mean achievement) until approaching school when Jenny suddenly got lively and pushed Arthur, Arthur pushed Jenny back, while I shied away. If I pushed would they push back? If I didn't push was I a sissy? Confusion stopped all activity till school.

To my surprise, English school wasn't all that different from Vienna except the atmosphere was less strict, and, instead of men teachers, there was a woman, a Mrs Bartlett. On my first day she told the children something very solemn about me. I didn't understand a word, but, whatever she told them, it turned me into a leper. At break (far more important than lessons) no one approached, no one touched, no one took the slightest notice of me. I looked for Jenny and Arthur as a foreigner looks for signs of his own language in a foreign country, but couldn't see them. I walked alone and was glad to be swallowed up in the classroom again. Only on leaving school did a human link appear as I followed the others into the sweet shop and, while tempted by Kit-Kat and Aero, watched the other boys, and, copying them, bought, with my halfpenny, four marbles: a glassy light blue, a milky red, a speckled yellow-green and dull grey. They dangled in a red net bag. It was these small glass balls that became both salvation and disaster by way of the international language of games. All the world's entrepreneurs, I'm sure, were marble cheats. It's competition gone rampant – you can win and win and never have enough; you can cunningly edge a marble closer with a foot or do a swap that leaves your rivals gasping at your gall; you can win a boy's favourite marble and see the tears well up in his eyes and glory at your power – you can then, in an act of splendid generosity, give the marble back and be thought a splendid fellow. Howard Hughes, Paul Getty, Richard Branson must all have been marble geniuses.

I hoarded mine. I waited. I watched the boys' incredible skill and sleight of hand, and I practised in quiet corners. Then, one day, heart-thumping, throat dry, face flushed, and barely able to see the encircling boys, I mimed that I wanted to have a go. There was a hush – the stranger had made a bid; the queer boy, so self-protectively alone, had joined in. I felt a warmth round me. Some were on my side – a cunning runt of a lad with a foxy face – had been winning too much. I bent down, and choosing the dull grey (the others were too precious) and screwing up my eyes, I sent it rolling. It hit one glass green. There were murmurs of approval. I picked up the won green, and, using the dull grey again, I cleaned up one more, and then lost my own by a miss. I was one up, so, strictly on a profit and loss basis, I put them back in my pocket and walked away. This was a mistake – you play and play until the bell goes; you don't hoard your own winnings – it was bad form. They did nothing – I simply felt the warmth ooze out of them – I'd broken a taboo. I was puzzled – what had I done wrong? Marbles is a hard game – the world in miniature. You learn more from them than saying your tables. In a few moments I'd been both popular and unpopular. To them I was still an enigma they weren't interested in solving – life was too rich and thrilling. I was an irrelevance until I had made my mark.

This came through a desperate effort to spell 'yes'. They were spelling all sorts of difficult words like stethoscope and enigma – I stumbled over 'yes'. Keeping strictly to phonetics, I wrote: J-E-I-S-S. Even the teacher – a kind enough soul – couldn't resist telling all and sundry about this. "Listen to this," she said, "Someone (they all knew who) "has spelt 'yes' J-E-I-S-S." At first there was silence, and then a titter, and then, seeing teacher smile, they all rolled about as though I was Charlie Chaplin. At first I was pleased – at least *some* attention was being paid to me. But then – when I heard the nature of the laughter – by now much exaggerated – I realised I was the butt of mockery – that they'd found a target and were making the most of it. But I'd made my mark – thereafter I was called 'Jeiss'.

I brooded. What to do? A fierce anger burned away. The world still swirled around me with only the occasional word making sense. These children were still strangers, but now I was no longer indifferent to them. I needed their interest, their companionship, and so I made yet another mistake, and, perhaps inevitably, it involved Jenny and Arthur.

I'd faithfully copied everything Jenny and Arthur did: their walking on walls, their swirling like aeroplanes and now a new game occupied us – Tick. You touched each other and then ran away – easy. And then, one day (the devil must have got into us) the touch became a bang, the bang a push, the push a charge – we were like devils; faster and faster, harder and harder, and then, suddenly, there was Jenny at my feet, staring up, both pain and a strange triumph in her eyes. And then an object flew towards me, a flying shadow, a face distorted with fury – it was Arthur. We hit at each other, arms flailing – I felt a knuckle on my cheek – and then, with all hell in me – I lashed and lashed, and there, joining Jenny on the pavement, he lay, his face averted and a trickle of blood from his nose. I was breathing hard and don't remember how I got to school – alone. Only then did I feel afraid, for, just before leaving Jenny and Arthur, I'd noticed the maid looking at us from across the road and then sliding into the house. *She* was bound to tell even if Jenny and Arthur kept quiet.

But as school absorbed me and Jenny and Arthur never came home with me, the incident receded, and I didn't quite realise its seriousness until late that night. In fact, lost in the fascination of the Cayman Island stamps, and, as the ritual at home in the evening seemed as before, I'd virtually forgotten Jenny and Arthur, until, having read my 25 lines (it was Treasure Island) – Dr Baum suddenly appeared by my bedside. I was pleased to see him and smiled at him. But he looked grave. He told me to put my book away and sat down on my bed, tilting it heavily towards him. Then began a slow, painful examination of what I thought 'fair' and 'unfair'. How did I think girls were to be treated? "She hit *me*!" I protested. He didn't change his grave expression. He said: "It was a game," and "in games you touch but don't hit." "But she hit *me* first!" I said and could feel the tears well up. My words had no effect on him – he simply went on about getting on with my 'friends', that they'd offered to escort me to school; that they were well-brought up children, and – here came the crunch – that I was bigger than they were.

I looked towards the orange curtains as though seeking help from them. I was utterly confused. I saw myself through Dr Baum's eyes – a large boy, fists straight out and two flailing bodies falling away. I'd been faintly proud of my 'victory', and now here it was in all its shame: I'd used the advantage of bigness; I'd been unfair, caused pain. And then, looking him straight in the eyes, I saw his dislike. The man put up with me, went for walks with me, sometimes explained this or that, but he didn't *like* me. So I turned to the wall, and now, despite trying, couldn't keep my tears back. I tried to stem the flow, and did, to some extent. He waited until I'd calmed down a bit, and then, coming closer to me, he said: "You know who behaves like that, don't you?" I shook my head.

"The Nazis."

Having scored the most damning of points, he got up and left the room, leaving me now not knowing what anything was – the world a completely bewildering place. I turned out the light and looked at the ceiling, and there, in the froth of gloom, I saw the image of Jenny and Arthur on the floor and recalled the moment of confusion and panic, and I thought: 'Never, never will I understand these people'.

Chapter 12

Dotheboys Hall

Soon after this event my life with the Baum's came to an end. Mrs Baum and I never got on. There was no point of contact – I was not the boy she had hoped for and she was too cold for me – she lacked that motherly femininity I was used to from Vienna. Anyway, I wanted to be near mum. So, heaven knows how, she found me a place in a small boarding school in Southborne (near Bournemouth).

The owners were two fat, spinster sisters with sharp eyes and sharper tongues. If I couldn't spell a word I was locked in the library with its glass cupboards until I found a book with the word in. I didn't mind being shut in the library for it was peaceful and I was away from the danger of the boys. They were tough, brutal and knew the survival game, though I was spared real bullying because they had Hugo to taunt and tease. Hugo was another refugee who was smaller than me and a born victim. With me, his only friend, he would bravely suppress his perpetual tears, and say, amidst gulps, "Let's play Monopoly." This terrific game was our main escape, and, over the board, we seemed to be fierce competitors, until I realised Hugo was always letting me win. The savour went out of the game after that.

In the afternoon, a snake of boys, led by a lumpy young woman, made its way to the beach. We slid branches along brown, slatted fences, making a fine noise, we pushed and shoved each other, so that, for safety's sake, Hugo would always stay right at the back and I would loyally walk with him. But, once on the beach, I broke free from his slightly oppressive friendship for I wanted to be 'one of the boys', that is, until I realised that the boys' instant disappearance on the beach was due to their having found a beach hut full of goodies. They had broken in and were stuffing their pockets with jars of mouth-watering jam, chocolate biscuits, bits of cake and so forth. They'd eat these at tea, offering us none, and watching our hungry eyes staring at food the like of which we could only dream about. There was no supervision at tea, indeed, supervision was minimal. It was expensive, so, boys' law ruled the place, with a lithe, athletic, good-looking South African, as leader. He was the main thief and the instigator of most activities like football in the dusty yard with a tennis ball – a bruising game I loved, for here at least, I was on equal terms with the others. Hugo was left staring mournfully at us from the side-lines and impatiently waiting for the game to finish. "Why do you play with them?" he asked plaintively. I didn't answer, for I knew, and, to a degree, enjoyed his envy of my stronger limbs and football skills.

Poor, poor Hugo. His integration into this country would be painfully slow, he was too timid, looking beaten before he was attacked.

The nadir of his existence at this modern Dotheboys Hall was when, coming home from the beach, at the back of the snake as usual, he whispered to me: "I want to go." "Go where?" "Toilet, you fool!" "Oh dear," I said. He walked faster, past the boys at the back. There were a few shouts of "Eh, what d'you think you're doing!" But Hugo had become desperate. I followed him, he rushed past the front boys, past the lumpy girl and I went with him. Yes, he reached the wide gate – only the round lawn at the front of the house surrounded by clean white pebbles, to go. He was walking incredibly fast when it happened – a drop of brown appeared beneath him, and then he stopped, and now the drop became a pool of liquid brown. The others caught up with him, and, with delight, they giggled and smirked. Hugo was led away by the girl and vanished into the school.

I saw him in the evening, down the end of a long corridor, arms deep in the sink, washing his clothes in brown water. He turned to face me, and, instead of tears, I was surprised to see anger: "The rubbish they are giving us here has given me diarrhoea," he said, and rubbed his clothes harder. I respected this reaction and liked him for it.

But there could never be equality between us, for, apart from differences in character, I had my mum only a trolley-bus drive's away and sad Hugo had no one. Once a week I could see her, once a week there was light in my life.

Chapter 13

The Tulip

Today I'd be seeing mum. She was my dream, my only dream, as I crunched over the clean gravel and through the wide open gate that led to freedom!

The journey to Bournemouth was to be savoured, as, secure in my seat on the yellow trolley-bus, I knew that, all too soon, I'd be on another bus going the other way, back to school.

Meanwhile I had two precious hours!

The details were of no importance – what we did or said didn't matter – her comforting presence would be by my side.

Both of us would hug secrets, neither of us would talk of them. I simply *couldn't* tell her of the misery of echoing corridors, the depressing dark green paint, the fear of danger at every corner – and I'd never, never tell her of the dark-blue steel cocoa cup we were handed every night, with the undrinkable purple-brown liquid inside it, the cup that symbolised a wretched existence. No, I'd keep my lips shut for there was nothing to be done about it. She could never afford a better boarding-school and she herself was trapped in that large house owned by the Misses Fisher, with Ilse – dark, mad, childless Ilse – who stared at me with hungry eyes – her companion servant.

Mum made me spend more of my precious time with Ilse than I wanted to, for Ilse made me uneasy; poor, barren Ilse, bony, intense, who seemed to devour every movement of mine. Ilse, who when the bell tingled a command: 'Come up here, the Misses Fisher want their tea' would swear in German and give a high-pitched mocking laugh. "The bitches want their tea," she'd say, rising, and mum and I would be left alone. There'd be a shy stare from her and a shy stare from me. But, with Ilse absent, the atmosphere would ease, the atmosphere in which we'd play a game in which we'd say nothing and everything.

"You OK?" she'd ask.

"Yes, I'm OK," I'd lie, "What about you?"

"Everything's fine," she'd lie. Then, "Wait a minute," she'd say, and left me alone while she went upstairs to change into her 'going-out' clothes – always the same blue dress and brown cardigan, carefully preserved for Saturdays when she and I were free.

I didn't mind being left alone to survey the large – nearly all-wood – kitchen and the splendid view of the carefully tended garden – so neat and square and tidy – with lawn edges cut with hardly a blade out of place – only the Municipal Gardens beat its sharp edges, the Municipal Gardens in which we'd soon be walking – carefully keeping our distance – for there was a fear of contact which might any moment dissolve into unseemly hugs, and – heaven help us – pent-up tears.

But why tears when we were so happy, for, while we were meeting from our two different worlds, here was time spent together! Our minds may not have been at one as they had been in Vienna, but there was love in the silence we shared.

Even in only my fourth visit we'd already dropped into a ritual. There'd be the trolley-bus from Parkstone, quietly humming its electric way into town, each moment stored up so it wouldn't be wasted. Our destination was known – the oval bustling town centre, but it was time spent together that counted, and she, her physical presence of indescribable comfort, would stare ahead without anxiety, quietly taking in this strange country. She was at peace, as I was – the only anxiety being the shortness of my stay. Yet even this was somehow stretched out as we were beginning to enjoy the habits and memories of my previous visits. "Look, you can already see Bobby's!" I pointed. Bobby's was the climax of our time spent together – the large, grand store at the heart of Bournemouth – the splash of elegance and expense, the place where she was not a servant and I not a poor schoolboy, and we'd walk, slowly, drinking in the sight of objects way out of our financial reach but symbolising a different life – a life to which, God willing, we might one day aspire.

But not yet, not yet Bobby's; first the Municipal Gardens – nearly all green but with bright, glowing splashes of colour – especially tulips standing to attention. Here we'd dawdle, and here there was danger of a hug. This would be uninhibited on her part but slightly embarrassing to me for I was at an awkward age – barely nine – when all show of affection was anathema. But I saw it as a return to our past, and, it, with its accompanying odour of mum, were to stay in my mind forever. In a way, it was my concession to love and I knew better than to show my shyness at this intimacy. I suppressed even the slightest negative movement, the slightest sign of aversion.

But today, as we sat in the garden, there was embarrassment at having nothing to say. We'd stored up and suppressed too many secrets; we'd been too long apart and got too involved in our new lives: we hadn't been together *enough*.

To break the silence, mum suddenly said, surprisingly:

"Ilse needs a child," and she gave me a sideways look. I sensed that she felt superior to Ilse because she had me, and I didn't like this. Ilse – even I realised – was a sad case, and I didn't think it was fair of mum. I wished she hadn't spoken and she sensed my thoughts and became embarrassed. Besides, I didn't want Ilse here in any shape of form – I wanted our intimacy to be exclusive, to eliminate all sad and horrible things: let us simply enjoy –

Was it this – this slight disruption of our mutual happiness – that caused me to get up and walk round the bench so I was momentarily out of sight of mum? She didn't move, staring straight ahead of her, lost in her own thoughts?

Behind the bench were some splendid red and yellow tulips – each flower in its own patch of rich brown earth – nature under control yet splendid in its glory. Mum had her back to me, and some instinct, some inner prompting, perhaps to repair any damage her remarks might have made, pushed me into looking right and left to make sure I wasn't being watched. Then I stooped down to grasp the base of a red tulip and tried to break it. But the sap prevented a clean break. I twisted it again, but still it wouldn't break, and then, with a very sharp twist, I managed it. I looked up in fear because for the first time in my life I'd stolen something, but everyone was some distance away and engrossed. So I carried my trophy, with its frayed stem, round the seat and stood in front of mother, holding the flower towards her as a present. She looked up – at first unaware of what had happened – then panic came into her eyes.

"Where did you -?" she stopped. Ridiculously I bowed a little and held the tulip out to her. At first she seemed unable to take it. Then, tears slowly welling up, she took it and turned her head away. Our discomfort was mutual and our eyes avoided meeting. I heard myself say: "Let's go to Bobby's now." She nodded and got up and we went to Bobby's and there began chatting, over-eagerly, about this and that. Perhaps, one day, we speculated, we'd be able to afford a very small item. And, in the café on the top floor, I looked forward eagerly to the selection of cakes where I always chose a chocolate eclair.

Mother and me, prim and proper in Bournemouth

Jack, the English schoolboy, complete with uniform

Chapter 14

Nearly A Catholic

Of course, mother was only too aware of my misery at the school. Hard as I tried not to talk of it, I transmitted it by every gesture, every movement. But there was nothing she could do about it. Her wages were pathetic and there was no help from British Jewry, nor from the state. Unexpectedly, help did come from the Quakers and from Catholic foundations. It was probably from these sources that I was found a place in Parkstone with the Moore family – the first real British family and the first place I was really happy. The contrast with the school could hardly be greater. There was only one problem – they were fervent Catholics.

The Moore's house gave no indication of the faith of its occupants – no holy statues, no pictures of the Virgin, not even a cross on the wall – they were muted, middle-class Roman Catholics who'd come to the faith by way of conversion from Protestantism. But if they didn't advertise their faith, they were ostentatious about their music: Uncle Frank was cathedral organist, his wife, Susan, was the cellist in a trio, and Dorothy, the red-haired darling of their union, was being taught both piano and cello.

They seemed, to me, to be constantly busy. Either he was practising the organ or inventing yet another perfume (he was a pharmacist) with a nice line in 'Moore's special after-shave'. Aunt Sue was always doing something 'artistic'. What delighted me most was 'collecting expeditions' in the woods round Bournemouth. We searched for beautiful, perfectly-shaped cones that could be coloured silver or gold and hung on the Christmas tree. I loved these outings.

Now Christmas had always been a happy event, even in Vienna, even if you were Jewish. It was the glowing heavily bedecked shops that did it. In early December, Chanukah time, they were alight with white St. Nicholas statues and brilliant red devil figures – both competing for our souls. Chestnut sellers wafted the air with their delicious smell, pavements seemed shinier, music came from everywhere and people *seemed* happier.

Yet, despite all this glamour, it didn't compare with the Moore's Christmas because for the first time I was part of it, I was with a family that was determined to squeeze every nuance of joy from the festival. Whilst Auntie made present-buying and tree-dressing major events, Uncle was off practising the organ. Presents were thought about weeks before and piled up under the tree in small hills of temptation. The whole family rehearsed carols round the piano, with me trying to keep up. I felt a little confused, a little bewildered, but, like any child, I was soon caught up in what amounted to a sort of annual hysteria.

The climax of all this was Midnight Mass. Now all those preparations would bear fruit. The tree was over laden, the presents all ready, but first we were off, in the bitter cold, to the cathedral, where Uncle Frank would perform his marvels. By pleading, I was allowed to stand by the organ and watch. Never had I seen Uncle more alive – he seemed all arms and legs. His face was thrust forward, he created music while looking up, now and then, at the mirror above his head that showed him what was going on at the altar behind him. The place was so full that steam rose from the crowd. They didn't seem to pay much attention to the service, busily chatting away, while Uncle, unconcerned, played on, and I was proud to be linked to such an important man.

Home we went through the echoing streets. It was thrilling to be awake at such an hour – at least one to two o'clock. Dorothy and I had never been up that late. The presents were beckoning – the eager tearing of paper – the delight or disappointment of what we would get – enviously watching each other, and then, I realised that Dorothy got much more than me, and I became uncomfortably aware that *she* was their child while I was … well, what? This was a problem. Aunt Susan tried so hard to include me in the warm circle of their family, yet I sensed the difference. I knew that come what may I was never *quite* a member of the family, and so, to compensate, I demanded *more* than my fair share – I demanded preference, until, one dreadful, day, Aunt shouted in frustration: "You want it all, don't you! Right, we'll leave, you can have this place. It's no longer ours, it's yours – you can have the lot!"

I was chastened and sorry and confused. Was I a real son of theirs or not? Obviously not, and Dorothy was not my sister. This was a bitter blow for we'd become good playmates. We played 'doctor and nurse' and even decided that "I'll show you mine if you'll show me yours". I remember my disappointment at the simplicity of little girls – there's so little to see! Also I itched to play the night errant to Dorothy's damsel in distress. Unfortunately she was so aggressive that she never needed my help, so I didn't get the chance.

But when it came to fighting, there was always Cookie. He was a flushed red-cheeked boy who was my friend, and firm friends we were!

He'd invited me to his small terraced house where his dad, an engine driver, talked to me of the glamour of flying sparks on the footplate – of roaring engines carving a trail of light and romance through south England.

Like Robert in Vienna, Cookie was the charismatic leader. He'd challenge a gang of toughs and shout back over his shoulder: "Come on, Jackie, you've got a good pair of fists!" Who can resist such a challenge!

But Cookie's real daring came out in violin classes run by Sister Gerard who somehow managed to cradle the small violin in the numerous black folds of her habit and got us scraping away and making a terrible noise. But the real attraction was Mary who had the roundest face and most mischievous of eyes. Cookie was hopelessly in love with her and would gaze at her dreamily. He wouldn't discuss her – his passion was too deep for words, but, one day, in the large school hall, when Sister Gerard, worn out by our lack of talent, had left us to practice, he somehow got into an animated conversation with Mary. It was obviously not the subject they were talking about that was of real interest – it was their mutual attraction. And, suddenly, Cookie could bear it no longer – he put his fleshy arms round Mary and gave her a huge, noisy kiss on her cheek, and then, overcome by his daring, he turned tail and fled. Mary's face was a deep red, while I just gawped at Cookie's courage, at his daring, at the sheer gall of it all. Instantly he became my number two hero. (Robert, in Vienna, was still my number one).

Despite my occasional unease at my position in the Moore family, I was very happy there. Also I was attracted by their faith. Of course I went to a Catholic school, St. Bernards, and went with them to mass. If I couldn't indulge in all the ritual, I could pray fervently and number my rosary and sense the presence of 'God' who I did not distinguish from the Jewish one. I was ready for religion and this one was at hand, the Jewish one was not. To all this, mother, on her monthly visits, said nothing.

The statue of the Virgin Mary in the local church became my solace. I could 'talk' to her, I could confess and acquaint her of my fears and hopes. Her serene face I thought beyond beauty. To add to all this there were the shimmering candles, the smell of incense, the priest's robes and the stern black and white morality I needed as guide-lines for my behaviour.

Only hell caused me problems: how do you 'burn forever', how implacable and cruel it seemed to me. So in bed, in the dark, the reality of hell was palpable and the tortures terrifying. I did recognise the 'thrill' of danger there hung about hell – it was the complement of heaven, and while in the daytime the attractions of the faith dominated, at night it was hell that reigned. 'Thank goodness' I thought, 'there's always purgatory – that's where I'm destined.'

I became fanatical in my devotions. I would get up at 5 o'clock in the morning, go the mass through the rain, and when the church was shut because the priest was unwilling to get up that early, I complained bitterly the next day to Sister Gerard. I learnt everything there was to learn and became the one who tested other children. Yes, I was ripe for the plucking, except for the fact that mother came visiting.

She was happy that I was happy. On her day there I did my chores perfectly – all the knives and forks laid correctly. I amused Aunt Susan by reciting to myself: "Fish forks on the outside ..." and so on.

After dinner mother and I would go walking. No longer was I neurotically dependent on her, instead I would recite events important to me: "Father Francis asked me to listen to a German broadcast on the school radio and translate for him. Afterwards he put his arm round my shoulders and said: 'Don't worry, the Germans won't get here.' I said I wasn't in the least worried – I knew that England would stop the Germans."

Then we climbed a hill, paved in short steps, and suddenly mother burst out bitterly: "You're no longer a Jew." It was like a blow in the face. I stopped climbing and sat down on the paved cobbles. I bowed my head and all my 'Catholic' acts flickered before me. I sensed the truth of her remark, and, because it was true, I burst out vehemently: "I am a Jew, I am a Jew!" and punched my knee. She said nothing, her words had been enough. I saw myself as a traitor to my religion, bitterly regretting my enthusiasm for Catholic ritual. I 'saw' Sister Gerard's kind face, 'felt' Father Francis' arm around my shoulders, and thought of them now as seducers. The picture had changed – they'd tried to capture me and all but succeeded and I felt bitterly resentful.

I continued going to St. Bernards, still yearned to be Dorothy's knight errant and went on with the Catholic ritual, but now with less enthusiasm – there was caution, there was doubt.

I had heard Chamberlain's famous broadcast while I was in a newspaper shop "... we are now at war with Germany." I was overjoyed – at last we were fighting – no longer would the monster be able to swallow one country after another. I thrilled to the war.

Disappointingly, at home life didn't change all that much, until, one day, mother appeared, looking serious. It seemed aliens would no longer be allowed to live by the sea – the fear was espionage. Mother would have to move to somewhere inland. But where would I go? They all looked at me and I didn't hesitate: "I'm going with mum," I said and her eyes glistened with tears.

Upstairs, in my room, I felt sick. I would have to leave all this – no comfortable home, no Dorothy, no Uncle and Aunt. then Uncle Frank entered my room. He sat down on the bed and said solemnly: "You'll soon be back; this war won't last long."

It was kind of him, and, for all I knew, he may even have believed it, and, for a while, the dream of returning to the Moore's stayed with me. Then, when it didn't materialise, it receded into memory.

Chapter 15

Little Austria

Our first port of call after the Moore's was Westbourne Terrace, Paddington. Here, behind these Georgian facades, the place had been turned into little Austria. The paint may have been peeling on the columns outside, but inside, the Viennese refugees chatted in German and in their tiny restaurant ate schnitzel and apfelstrudel. They pretended neither war nor Nazis existed. But where to put a nine year-old boy? With the women, of course: what harm can he do?

So there I was, stuck at the very end bed so that I saw as little as possible. But I saw enough as I glimpsed delightful cameos of women unselfconsciously taking off their stockings, straightening their skirts and doing even more intimate things. The smell delighted me – it was the irresistible feminine odour that projected the mystery of womanhood. Even a nine year-old had to respond to such secret delight. The downside was the older women, they were sad with their sagging flesh, and I vowed, then and there, that I would never grow old.

There was great excitement when a particularly beautiful woman had been asked out by a young Austrian. The other women pressed on her their best clothes, gave freely of their make-up, and she became a symbol that normal life continues no matter what and that elegant Vienna can survive in London. The girl got more and more nervous as the climactic date got nearer. Then, all the women squeezing together at the window, saw the two meeting. They giggled at her shyness, they all but cheered as she came close to him and the two held hands. The girl must have been only too aware of her audience on the second floor and quickly took her paramour away, but not before even I got a glimpse of a couple defying the desperate state we were all in, for, whatever fun we were having, we had to find jobs quickly so that every day we searched newspapers, queued at agencies and grasped at any straw.

Downstairs, in the small hall, a drama company was formed, and, responding to the magic of the stage for the first time, I witnessed a play about putting on a play, and recall, to this day, what I thought was a hilarious joke. The optimistic producer said to the dramatist: "Look, they're streaming in to see your play." The playwright, a gloomy fellow, looking down at the theatre's entrance said: "Yes, I can see one streaming in now." Thus was triggered my delight in the human comedy. Ever since, I've been telling that joke to anyone who cared to listen.

It was extraordinary how happy we were for a short time – a real Viennese play and real Viennese food. In a way, we never wanted to leave little Austria. But, shortly before mother found a job in Leicester, I was spotted by a school inspector, playing my favourite game of shooting up the 'German army panzers' going past on Westbourne Terrace. This game, made vivid by my over-active imagination, was very satisfactory. A thick tree branch did for the barrel of the gun and was wedged between two round boulders which served for wheels. Placed strategically in the forecourt, I imagined Robert, my Viennese friend, to be by my side. He loaded the gun (I was the commander), and we peppered the passing traffic; not a panzer escaped our withering fire.

Mother was always thrown into a panic by authority. So: "Yes, of course he'll go to school, Mr Inspector." "A Catholic one," I insisted, remembering my good time at St. Bernards. "OK, a Catholic one." St. Barnabas it was, and so small was the school, that several ages were in one room. And there, thrust before my eyes by Sister Percival was a book with tiny print about a bearded man who'd lent some money to a mighty grand person who didn't pay it back. I thought: 'Of course the bearded one wants his money back. Who wouldn't!' But no, no, he was condemned by everyone: he was called heartless, without mercy, a real devil! As he was a Jew, I felt uncomfortable, and noticed Sister Percival looking at me with a gleam in her eye. But then I read the Jew's plea: 'If you prick us do we not bleed ...' and my love flowed out to the writer and has remained with him ever since. Even if the world was unjust, such humanity redeemed all.

But, like all idylls, our stay in little Austria had to come to an end. In a newspaper mother saw an advertisement for a companion /

servant in Leicester. Immediately the idea of a 'companion' attracted her – she thought it was a step up from being a mere servant. The 'servant' part was clear enough – you cleaned and cooked and treated everyone with great deference, but the 'companion' part, what was involved there? We soon found out.

Chapter 16

Mrs Adams

The afternoon ritual always began with preparing the silver tea tray. Mother never let me help her as the slightest deviation, the smallest of mistakes, led to ructions. All the handles of the Worcester cups had to face the same way, the gleaming super-white napkins had to be placed precisely by their side; cake knives were highly polished, as were the Apostle spoons. Exactly at 4.30 – not a minute sooner or later – we made our way from the flagstoned gloomy kitchen to cross into the red carpeted area where feet sank in, and walked up to the shiny nut-brown door of the lounge.

Mum knocked deferentially – a knock always answered at the *third* go – never the first or second – by the command "In" from the cracked 88-year old voice of Mrs Adams.

I kept well behind mum to spare myself even two seconds of the trial of our afternoon tea with its appalling silence interrupted only by the tinkle of cups and the ever-ticking clock. The only conversation I ever got was: "Don't spill crumbs on the carpet."

I sat sideways to Mrs Adams, for, having, on our arrival, sat right in front of her, she'd said sharply: "I can't keep staring at that child. You -" she pointed a crabbed finger at me, "Sit here," indicating the armchair to her left. I tried hard to avoid looking at the side of her face for it filled me with hate. Her hair was the only attractive feature, pure white, piled high by the weekly hairdresser – one of our very rare visitors. I could see only the cracks on her white over-powdered face and ribbed neck, the rest was all black. Mum had been tutored to pour out English tea and not to spill a drop for then poor mum would have to go back to the kitchen and fetch a new cup and saucer.

To relieve my boredom I stared hard at the privet hedge, the only thing to be seen out of the large window, and concentrated on the point where a tangle of branches spread out. I imagined it to be rivers flowing from the main branch, and thought of it as the Nile delta flowing into the empty hole beneath the branches that was the Mediterranean.

Then came the ritual command: "You may have some cake now." Battenburg was my favourite for I could break it into four and eat each quarter slowly to spin out the time – time doled out through clock ticks, time hanging heavily, time conquered by imagination.

The final ritual was: "You may clear up now," and mother would carefully collect cups, plates and so on, trying to make as little noise as possible. She'd leave first and I'd follow – out on to the flagstones and into the freedom of 'our' kitchen where we could get down to books and intimacy. But even here we'd have to keep our voices low for the house echoed and any signs of laughter would bring rebuke from Mrs Adams, and, perhaps, God help us, prompt a visit from her. If she ever came she'd contaminate our kitchen, she'd poison the loving relationship between mum and me, where I, yes *I*, taught mother English words – words culled from my only book – Treasure Island – now in its fourth reading – a book that made irrelevant the kitchen gloom, that banished Mrs Adams, and even temporarily banished from consciousness mother's beloved but ever-worried face. The silence of the house had infected even us – for we rarely chatted with ease, and here I sensed my inadequacy, for hadn't this nervous woman, so thin, so tense, once happily gossiped with friends and relations in Vienna? A woman who'd glowed with life, but was now reduced to being a servant / companion to this monster in the lounge. I knew she'd talked to Aunt Marie or Aunt Irma as she could never speak to me. But I tried to make up by teaching her and by asking questions about Mrs Adams. "Hasn't she *any* friends?"

Mother's eyes sparkled with schadenfreude, "No, none."

"How did she get this large house?"

"Her husband left it her."

"What was he?"

I imagined a tycoon or banker, but no – and mother couldn't resist a giggle, "He was a butcher." Now we both giggled and I tried to imagine *Mr* Adams, arms bloodstained, raising a large butcher's cleaver about to decapitate an unfortunate animal, a man who'd once been married to this ancient, over-dressed, finicky and snobbish wife. They didn't fit.

But one day there was a change in our lounge ritual for I was told by Mrs Adams to leave the room *on my own*. Nervously I negotiated the lounge furniture and left, leaving mother behind. What was going on? I could hear voices but not what they said. I listened, bravely putting my ear to the gleaming mahogany door. Mumble, mumble, and then I thought I could hear a raised anxious voice, my mother's, followed by the lower inexorable mumble of Mrs Adams. Suddenly the door opened, I stepped guiltily back, but mother didn't notice me – she rushed past me – into the sanctuary of the kitchen. I ran after her, and then, on the over-scrubbed kitchen table, she lay her head and sobs shook her, heaving sobs, but quiet ones – more eerie than outright sobbing.

"What is it?"

"We have to leave."

My mind became a whirl: what *had* I done? And I burst out: "I wiped my shoes on the mat, I never said a word in the lounge and I didn't drop any crumbs -"

I was engulfed in mother's arms. "It's not your fault, darling, you've been perfect. It's me."

"But what have *you* done?"

"She says I didn't dust the banisters."

"But you did!"

"I know I did." Now mum had a peculiar smile on her face, "It's something else, something between women -"

"But what?"

"You see," she said and lowered her voice, "Mrs Adams never had children ..."

"So it *is* me!" I cried.

Suddenly mother became hysterical: "It's not you – never think that. Promise me you'll never think that – you're not to blame for anything. You understand – ?"

I nodded.

"You're *sure* you understand?"

I nodded again.

She seemed satisfied and then I saw her shoulders slump and the energy seemed to go out of her: "Now leave me alone. I'm going upstairs." And she left the kitchen.

I thought: Where do we go now? Where can mum get another job? This place, this awful place, may be a kind of prison but it is somewhere to live. There is this kitchen, and, upstairs, our room .... We had enough difficulty finding this place. A servant with a ten year old child can hardly pick and choose, and especially a refugee servant whose English was poor and aroused suspicious glances in wartime England because of her German accent. I itched to take up Treasure Island and escape, but was frozen into inaction by a sense of helplessness. I was enraged by our vulnerability, by our being at the mercy of the likes of Mrs Adams. Confused in thought and feeling, I thought I heard, at a far distance, a thin, high sound, but ignored it, then slowly into consciousness came the same sound, a little clearer, and it was my name, 'Jackie!'

I rushed into the hall, and there mum lay at the bottom of the steps in a heap. Panic froze me while she looked helplessly into my eyes.

"I can't move," she mumbled, "all dizzy."

Despite my panic and fear that she might die, a strange joy came into me – this was my turn, my turn to be grown-up, to lift her up, to get her up those stairs to our room. But it was a clumsy business – she was too heavy to carry, of course, but with my arm round her and hers round my shoulders, we staggered upstairs, step by step. Despite my desperation, I thought: 'This is one of life's trials – can I manage and afterwards feel a hero?'

Half way up a dreaded voice said sharply from below: "What do you think you're doing!"

I shouted: "Doctor – get a doctor!"

"Answer me, woman, and you, boy, what are you up to?"

"She's ill – can't you see!"

"Don't be ridiculous!!" It was almost shouted – a kind of frustrated fury.

Despite my burden I half turned my face and saw her in all her terrifying frailty – trying so hard to deny all humanity in herself. My hate reached a new peak and I shouted at her: "Get a doctor you – you ..." and then I spat out, "you butcher's wife!"

I saw a change in her – a shadow pass across her face, and, without another word, she went into her room and banged the door on us.

We got upstairs, but just before I lowered mum on the bed she gave me a kiss on my temple – a warm kiss, and I also saw a small smile of triumph – that between us – together – we'd conquered yet another adversary. Hitler couldn't destroy us – nor could Mrs Adams.

Chapter 17

The Coopers

War-time restrictions eased when the potential 'spies' among the refugees had been safely interned in the Isle of Man. Some didn't waste their time on the island – the Amadeus String Quartet was formed there. The others were now allowed a little more freedom, mother no longer had to report to the police so frequently and, best of all, she was permitted to take up other work than domestic service. Instantly she looked for a job in accounts. She loved numbers, enjoyed the tidiness of neat columns and nearly always fell a little in love with her boss. People quickly appreciated her skill, they felt her to be utterly trustworthy and knew she had the firm's interest at heart. It was Sorrel and Co., estate agents, who took her up and she stayed with them for years to become a family friend and visit them in their luxury home in Kirby Muxloe. Meanwhile I'd won a scholarship to the Wyggeston and threw myself into the school's academic and sports sides. The place prided itself on being Leicester's most prestigious school and you were liable to get a bit of stick from the other children wearing the black and silver uniform in town. But I didn't care – I was proud of the uniform and there was little doubt in my mind that we *were* superior. I'd become a bit of a prig.

But with hindsight I know how much I owed the school – above all, I absorbed its public school values, and, just as I'd thrown myself almost fanatically into the beliefs and strictures of the Catholic Church, now this snobbish place had an eager and pliant pupil. It's prefects, at the time the Attenboroughs were two of the prefects, and sports captains were heroes, its academic efforts took up most of my evenings with homework. I absorbed its maths and science, but most of all its history and English through the efforts of a kindly and civilised teacher called Mr George. Here, perhaps, questioning began. Reading Hugh Walpole's 'The Cathedral' showed me how fragile and vulnerable institutions such as cathedrals could be. If one of the main efforts of a school should be to arouse questioning in the minds of its pupils, the Wyggeston, via dear Mr George, didn't do badly.

I was more susceptible to the school's ethos than many others because I had few other values to pit against its powerful teaching. Sadly, Judaism was not being nourished by mother because she'd lost all contact with the community. Besides, she regarded them as a snobbish lot with little interest in refugees. So, she resorted to simplicities – I was to be a well mannered boy who believed in the ten commandments – not bad as far as it went, but not enough for a boy needing a framework for his life, urgently in need of guidance. So, I became a fervent Wyggestonian, laying, quite unconsciously, and paradoxically, the foundation for a later wide and avid questioning of everything and anything. First came firm values, later came iconoclasm.

But, Wyggeston or not, we had to have somewhere to live. Not easy for a woman with a son on the verge of puberty. With her usual tenacity, mother cast round far and wide, and, as luck would have it, she found a place with the Coopers in Wigston – a good-natured but incompatible baker and his wife who were badly in need of children. So, as with the Baum's, I found myself as a kind of quasi-son, a substitute for the real thing, and, without any conscious awareness, I began to act out my role.

Hilda Cooper was Welsh and never let you forget it. You'd think Ebbw Vale, where she came from , was a kind of heaven, perhaps for her it was. But why ever did she come to Wigston, Leicestershire, *England*? "It was Doug," she said, "I fell for Doug," and she looked gloomily out of the window, a look implying that a dreadful mistake had been made, for which there was now no remedy.

Every day she'd serve Doug his inordinately large dinner. Neither would say a word. His mind was on the large hut up the garden path where he kept his menagerie of cavies, rabbits and beautiful strutting bantam fowls. He was already in his brown overalls, shovelling food, especially parsnips for which he had a fondness, into his mouth and ready to dash off.

Hilda, I knew, had her mind on the trifles she'd picked up in women's magazines and on her passion. This was quite simply to dance all day and night. I watched her once and she was brilliant. She had automatic rhythm, and, with a strong man's arms about her, she would float or swirl or throw her splendid legs into the eyes of all and sundry. On the dance-floor she was transformed from a very ordinary, not particularly good-looking woman, into a swirling beauty.

The trouble was there was only one dance a week in war-time Wigston and men tended to want to follow up a dance. Doug didn't seem to care. After an evening's work with his animals or in the garden, he went, exhausted, up to bed and snored contentedly. Hilda would sneak in between twelve and two and creep into bed. Mum and I listened to this routine, and, young as I was, I thought it strange that husband and wife could be so different. I thought it even stranger when Hilda, one day, grabbed me, and said: "Come here, boyo, I'll teach you to dance." And she did. Taking the lead, she pushed me this way and that, she thrust her legs round mine, unashamedly, she let her breast rest on my arm, and, gradually, a little of the fervour that impelled her, transferred itself to me. "You've got two left feet," she'd laugh, "but you'll do, you'll do." And, knowing she'd excited me a little, she began to hum the latest hit. For her life wasn't too bad with a pubescent boy to dazzle at home and the thrill of Saturday nights to look forward to.

But one Saturday night she was later than usual. Not that this woke Doug until she came through the front-door crying very loudly. Her cries woke him. She turned to sobbing and I heard them arguing, and then Doug said: "I knew this would happen, I just knew it. Blasted woman – what did you do?"

"Nothing."

"You must have done *something*!"

I couldn't hear her excuse and then Doug said: "Now I've got to go and sort it out." Then he shouted at her: "You're never going there again, d'you hear!"

She sobbed: "I won't Doug, I won't."

I had visions of large men waiting for Doug coming up to them, shouting: "Who called my wife a tart?" for I'd heard the words "called me a tart" from Hilda. I got out of bed. I put on my dressing-gown and went out on the landing. I looked down and saw Doug putting on his thick, grey raincoat, and said timidly, for really I was scared: "Do you want any help?" He looked up, and despite his troubles, he smiled: "No, you go back to bed." But just as he opened the front door, he shouted over his shoulder, "Thanks, Jackie."

Somehow it was sorted out. For a while Hilda didn't go dancing. But such was her misery that slowly she re-started. However, she came home earlier, she lowered her dress and wore far less make-up. That seemed to satisfy Doug. Somehow they managed to live together as man and wife.

* * * * *

My full integration into the Cooper household came with Doug giving me the tortoiseshell cavy to look after. She was called Julie, and, lovingly, I would scrape her pill-shaped droppings from the hutch floor. Then I'd sawdust the urine-sodden wood and gave her glistening yellow straw to muzzle into. Clean and beautiful, I'd watch the one living object that was officially 'mine'. Doug also shared his allotment with me and occasionally he talked about that great moment when, some time ago, he'd finished building his creosoted hut. "There it is," he said proudly, and pointed to a slab on the concrete floor on which was written in pebbles: 'Laid by Douglas Cooper, February 1941, finished August 1941'. It was quite a feat, this hut, and I knew he was planning another one. But, on the whole, he didn't talk much. It was a silent companionship and very satisfying – for me a change from the grind of homework, while he seemed happy in my sharing his kingdom.

Perhaps the climax of our relationship came with the arrival of Flossie. She was a small black and white fox terrier, very nervous, very eager and very loveable.

Though really Doug's dog, I found myself playing with her more and more. I'd take her up to the allotment and chuck clods of earth for her to chase, and when she found a rabbit hole and dug furiously into it I all but joined in.

Gradually she was following *me* rather than Doug, so, one day, having finished my dinner early and no homework to do, I got up and called to her: "Come on, Flossie!" and went outside. Without turning round, I knew she was following me, but then I heard Doug shout behind me: "You come *here*, Flossie!" He was almost snarling. The poor dog was caught between two forces, so I said: "Go back in Flossie – back to the house." She did and Doug slammed the door on me.

After this I would cuddle and tease her only when Doug was not in sight. But the secrecy of our affection only increased its intensity; in fact, when Doug was out of the way I could hardly keep my hands off her.

Then came a change in Flossie – she grew fatter and her movements became ungainly. I was ignorant of such things as pregnancy and Doug wasn't the type to talk of such embarrassing subjects. The nearest he got to any mention of Flossie's state was to get a nice box with a blanket in it and place it in the kitchen and say: "That's where she'll go when her time comes." He tried to get her used to the box but she'd have nothing to do with it and hid anywhere and everywhere in the garden for her rest. Usually I found these places and – whether asleep or not – I'd nag her into a caress. Sometimes she'd growl at me, but I missed her furry comfort so much I'd stroke her belly and speak loving words to her which she'd accept – but very reluctantly.

One day I came down to breakfast to hear someone scraping away just outside the backdoor. Looking out, I saw Doug anxiously bending down and scooping ash away from underneath the small dilapidated and unused shed which stood about a foot off the ground by the backdoor. Dust from the ashes arose round his legs and I knew what had happened – Flossie must have given birth beneath the shed – just about the most inaccessible place there was.

As soon as I got outside Doug was shouting at me: "Get some food for her – quick – we'll try and tempt her out." I did, and bending down to place the dish for her, I saw peeping out from the darkness two green eyes, wild with anger, staring at me – it was frightening.

"Come on, Flossie, EAT!" I entreated her. Only a growl. Doug said: "Let's move away and see if she'll come out – she must be starving. We moved back leaving the tempting dish there. Very slowly, very cautiously, we saw a pointed nose – now covered in black grime. She approached the dish, she sniffed, but kept jerking her head up to see if her 'enemies' were around. "Quick!" said Doug, rushing forward to try and grab her, but she was too fast for him and had rushed back to guard her pups. "She can't stop there," I said fearfully. "No, she can't" Doug muttered and went on: "She'll kill the pups – she'll lie on them." Close to tears, I said: "She doesn't know what to do!" Doug bit his lip. "Look, if you go round the back she'll move that way and then I'll go underneath on the other side and grab a pup and put it in the pregnancy box." Quite afraid of Flossie by now, I approached the shed, bent down and let her see my face. Wild with terror and anger, the green eyes blazed at me, the bared teeth were plain to see. This wasn't my beloved dog – this was a crazed animal responding to her deepest instincts. As Doug carefully approached from the other side – with sacking round his hands – she suddenly whipped round and buried her head in the sacking, biting hysterically and with such fury that I quailed. Doug retreated, the sacking torn to shreds.

For a moment he stood there, baffled, then said: "Let's have breakfast and give her time to calm down." so, much relieved, we returned to the kitchen and ate our food, saying nothing but thinking furiously. The pregnancy box stood empty and useless in the corner.

Hilda was crying. "Poor thing," she kept saying, until Doug, frustrated and anxious, told her to shut up.

After breakfast he'd made up his mind. "The shed will have to come down," he said firmly. "But she's underneath," I wailed. "We'll have to dismantle it bit by bit so she'll be exposed and we'll have a chance to grab a pup."

We worked together, both of us sweating more from anxiety than exertion. We complemented each other – he hacking up the nails, I pulling the plank away. We got into a rhythm, wrenching at planks and nails. Carefully we picked up the shards of glass so as not to hurt Flossie's paws. Now only the floor was left. We paused and listened. No sound. Had the noise of tearing the shed to bits terrified her into silence or was she dead? In desperation we tackled the floor, and then, to our relief, Flossie began to bite at bits of the wood as they were wrenched away; once she clung on to a bit and was lifted clean into the air before she let go. Slowly, she and her brood were exposed.

Bereft of cover, she curled herself round the pups; the ashes had discoloured all the animals and she was quivering with fear. I tried to see underneath Flossie and thought I saw five pups, and, thank goodness, one seemed to be alive and was clinging to her teat. "If only we can save one," Doug muttered. He got some fresh sacking and carefully approached from his side. I thought Flossie would be too exhausted and he could pick her up easily. But no, she charged the sacking, and, amidst the growls and yelps, he shouted at me: "Grab the pup!" But I stood there, paralysed. "Grab the pup!" Doug yelled at me. I plunged forward blindly, but was inept. I came away with nothing – but now Doug had enclosed the hysterical Flossie and carried her, clinging to the sacking, indoors, and banged the back door shut. I looked at the litter – only one of the pups was just about moving. Trembling, I picked it up – a barely warm bundle of fur – and carried it towards the kitchen. I held it up for Doug to see it through the door window, but then the bundle went limp in my hand.

"Never mind, give it here," Doug said, and carried it indoors. gently he placed it in the pregnancy box and gave it to Flossie. Instantly she began to lick it.

Flossie didn't last long – next day she was dead and Doug spared me the sight of her bedraggled and blackened body by burying it before I got up.

We couldn't talk about it – mutual guilt had silenced us: I cursed my demanding love, my pestering her, my lack of respect for her peace. You can love too much, I thought. But Doug never mentioned her and to his day I don't know what his thoughts were.

* * * * *

Was there anything between Doug and mum? Certainly there was a softness in his voice when he called her by name: "Stella". He was always most considerate to her and often I saw them deep in conversation, especially about money matters. His wife was incapable of adding two and two and instantly bored when anything serious came up. She'd say: "Oh, Doug, *you* know all about that, don't you," and pick up a magazine. Mother would sit down and take up his accounts book from work to unravel his numbers. Also, I realised later, mother had a sly sexuality that enticed without, apparently, any effort on her part. Men were drawn to her almost subconsciously. Also, there were signs that, after so many years of looking after me alone, she was becoming weary – yes, even of me. I was an emotional creature, altogether too clinging. I'd wait anxiously at the bus stop at home-coming time in order to see her loveable figure come out of the vehicle. Only then would my anxiety be eased. Only then would I be sure that there had been no accident or she hadn't walked out on me. I was becoming acutely aware that mother and son are not for eternity, that, strong as our ties were, there would come a separation. The result was that I clung to her even more tenaciously.

Things came to a head during the long summer holidays. Hilda simply couldn't handle me; Doug and mum were out at work. I was one of only two grammar school boys in the area – the other was Bill Maynard, Greengrass in Heartbeat – and I was soon bored.

Mum found a summer school for refugees, way out in Wem, Shropshire. So she sent me there. "Only for three weeks," she assured me. But for me, three weeks separation from her was an eternity.

Chapter 18

Escape from Wem

The dream told me quite clearly: 'My mother is dead'. A grim, black-coated man barred my way to her bedroom door. It was not to be opened for behind it was...

On waking in the dormitory where five others slept, I stared at the ceiling patterns, the dream more vivid than the waking world – that man in the black overcoat – the door behind which ...

I tried to move my limbs to get out of bed but was paralysed, and then a voice whispered: 'You don't *know* that your mother's dead; you've got to find out; the only real way is to hear her sweet voice on the 'phone, to hear her say all panicky: 'What's wrong? Are you all right? Why did you ring?' Of course pride would stop me saying: 'Because I dreamt you were dead.' No, I'd make up excuses: 'I'm bored here, or my best friend, Abram, has found someone else, or the food's lousy, or -' And then it would all burst out, the whole wretched misery: 'Can I come home early?' She'd sigh, I could almost 'hear' that sigh: 'Oh, Jackie, why do you ask? You know that Uncle Doug and I are out all day -'

'I know, I know,' I'd say.

'Are you *that* unhappy there?' she'd sigh again, and I'd try and reassure her: 'It's OK, it's OK – only a few more days to go -'

'You're sure, you're absolutely sure?'

'I'm sure,' and the 'phone would be put down with a whispered 'Bye, darling -' But at least I'd know she was alive – I'd know she was *there*. So a 'phone must somehow be reached! That meant asking the headmistress and I decided to do that at breakfast.

I got there early in order to sit near her, but talk at breakfast was difficult, and, besides, she had her favoured seniors to whom she usually chatted. I tried hard to gain her attention – smiling at jokes, listening to what they were saying, all the time my mind telling me: 'When the time comes, ask her quietly, sensibly and *don't* cry!' To my surprise, she suddenly turned to me: "And how are *you* getting on, Jackie?" Oh, how I wanted to tell her: 'I'm so homesick I think I'm ill and my mother died and is lying on that pink duvet ...' but all I managed was: "All right," and then, breathlessly, I said: "May I – Can I '?" "Can you what?" And out it came: "Can I 'phone home?"

"No!" It was so firm and sharp that I knew it was hopeless – no argument would break her down and her face showed a hardness that shut me out. She turned away from me and in that instant I knew I had no choice; now I knew what I was going to do.

Yet I hesitated all morning, aching to share my secret with Abram. We were mates of the type that told each other everything: our hate of this place, our longing for the soft comforts of home, and so on, and so on. We were bonded by misery, yet curiously happy in each others sadness and longing. But I knew I couldn't tell him this for he's bound to say: 'Don't be so daft – you'll be caught within a few miles.' Also, for all I knew, he might even give me away.

I was shrewd enough to wait for dinner to be over, for at dinner I might be missed. And then I ambled through the school's small wood, casually, as if just taking a walk. At the back of me the grey house, at the front, a path. I avoided it for I knew I was already on the run.

The gate stood completely open and empty. It was so EASY. All I had to do was put one foot in front of the other. Yet it meant crossing the barrier between what was allowed and what was forbidden and I'd been brought up to follow rules all my life. I edged towards the gate – just a bit of tarmac – and then I was through and the energy pumping into my legs. I walked fast, but not too fast for I might meet someone who would stare at a boy running away from school and report me to authority. I could just see the headmistress, frowning, saying down the line: 'A boy – yes – from the summer school – running away – that's right, he's probably heading for Wem station. Thank you, sergeant.' And now I suddenly realised I wasn't safe at Wem. It was only a tiny village with one dull station – the obvious place to start looking for me. But, anxious or not, I was suddenly happy, for I was no longer brooding on that door so far away. I had something else to think about and I was glad.

But when I read the Wem time-tables my heart sank: no train for two hours! The evening meal wasn't till six, an age away, but Abram was bound to ask someone: 'Where's Jackie?' and that would start off the hunt … No, Wem must be left behind. I looked for the next station down the line – Whitchurch. And, to my right I saw a road-sign saying: 'Whitchurch – 10 miles.' Ten miles is far away but one could imagine ten miles, one could 'see' them stretching down the road. So I set out, saying to myself: 'Whitchurch is safety – Wem dangerous' 'Whitchurch is safety – Wem dangerous.'

The method was good: a steady pace that would make me forget my legs; and it was very satisfying to see the ten become eight, then six and a half – I was conquering the hurdle of distance. But I hadn't reckoned with the enemy. It came with a few warning spots, then a great gust of wind. I had no raincoat, and, suddenly, I was a victim of water battering my head, of water splashing up my short trousers, of water on my bare knees. Being a townie I'd never met country rain: it seemed a thing of vengeance, creeping down my neck and even coming into my ears. And the sound wiped out everything – you could hear nothing but rain. I looked for an escape – a hedge? And then, behind the grey curtain of rain was a house. I thought of knocking at the door – but its stark, shut-up greyness put me off; besides the train at 6.43! There was no world, I thought, where dryness existed, and then another house and another – seen dimly as I glanced up quickly from my head hunched into my collar – and I knew that Whitchurch was not far away; and, with that thought, the rain eased. It was as if I'd passed a test and survived; I felt that now I could do anything.

Clothes drying on you make you itch in odd places. There were damp patches on my thighs which, I thought, would never go away. I pushed my full weight against the ticket office's huge door and entered the starkest room I've ever seen – only a green bench and bare floorboards and yellow-grey walls with cracks in them, and there, the double glass windows that would decide my fate.

I knew I had just enough money, but would anyone serve a miserable-looking boy asking for a ticket to Leicester? I knew I had to ask in a matter-of-fact voice, no wavering, no pleading. What if he said 'No' or 'What are you up to, sonny?' I could think of only one reply: 'My mother's dead.' I could hear my heart as I put my head just above the counter. No one there – an empty station – an empty ticket office. I coughed – I certainly hadn't the guts to bang a coin on the counter, and then a man appeared. "Yes?" he asked, looking bored. "Ticket for Leicester – one way," I said, and thought I'd said it quite evenly, not inviting any 'ifs' or 'buts'. He got a green ticket, banged it into the stamping machine and then hesitated. 'Here it comes,' I thought, 'the questions -' But "Money," was all he said – no doubt not expecting me to have any. But I had it and a few pence more. I shoved it through the gap, hoping my hand wouldn't tremble. He reached forward and offered the ticket. I told myself: 'Don't hurry, don't snatch.' So I took it calmly and felt an enormous victory. I walked away to the bench and sat on it with the precious ticket in my hand. I wondered if the world had been evacuated of all people except the man and myself.

Nor did the train to Crewe help, for, apart from having a compartment to myself, the rain started up again, wiping out the countryside. I wondered if a ghost was driving the train and I its only passenger. Stations came and went, no one seemed to get out or in, no doors banged. I hoped Crewe would be full of life, for I longed for signs of humanity, almost any humanity, for loneliness had invaded me.

At Crewe I got out and looked around. I stared up and nothing was there except an eternal ever-reaching blackness – punctuated only by very tiny lights like distant stars. Below these pin-points of light were faint pools of light on the platforms. Grey platforms – pool of light – grey platform – another pool. None of the station's rooms seemed occupied or lit; and then I saw him, my first sign of a human being apart from the ticket-man: a porter, slouching along, opening a door and disappearing. It was like a dream – one figure moving silently in that giant hollow of a station. But as I approached the centre of the place, things cheered up: there was laughter from somewhere, another man was sweeping the platform – a waste-bin had coloured wrappers in it.

The time-table showed me a one and a half hour wait before the big London express would take me to Nuneaton; then – what joy! - there, marked on the white paper, was the name 'Leicester'. There's magic in names if your loved one is at the other end, for, with the sight of the word 'Leicester' the reality of mother's existence came back to me and I all but rejected the message of the dream: Surely, she *must* be alive!

A voice by my side said: "You're going AWOL."

It was startling, I nearly jumped.

"Pardon?" – ever the polite boy.

"AWOL – that's what you are – absent without leave."

I looked at the RAF figure to my left, but he was so matter-of-fact about it that I found I wasn't at all shy with him.

"I might be," I said, just a bit cautious.

He nodded and returned to silence.

Then, "Well," he said, "happens all the time." He shrugged but didn't say he was AWOL – or why he was there. So he's holding back, I thought.

"Leave?" I asked bravely.

"That's right. Leave," and he laughed and stood up and stretched his arms and yawned mightily.

He said: "I'm going to Preston," and, to my surprise, he held out his hand and I took it.

Then he lowered his voice: "Good for you!" he said intimately and nodded encouragement. Then he jerked into action, "Come on, can't leave you here all night – let's explore –"

My spirits lifted – the damp, still on my clothes, seemed a trifle, the loneliness simply vanished and I thought the war, this night and this extraordinary empty station weren't so bad. 'Yes, let's explore,' I thought and we began to look into the dark nooks and crannies of this vast place.

One human being brought another, and, suddenly, there was a porter talking to the RAF man. They laughed. The RAF man pointed to me, the porter nodded, went away and came back with two iron bars. What was happening? He came towards us, holding one steel bar for me and another for the RAF man. "There's loads of 'em," the porter pointed to a dark patch at the back of the platform. "When they come out you wham 'em." And he left to go to the back of the dark patch.

"What do I wham?" I liked the feel of the iron bar though it was heavy. The RAF man grinned, but looked excited. He lowered his head and said with malice:

"Rats!"

Ye Gods – I was scared of rats – but the situation demanded manliness, courage *and* speed. So I stood there, iron bar grasped with both hands, and on the ready, but not too close to the hole – a mixture of fear and excitement. The RAF man stood opposite – we waited. Then the porter, somewhere to my right, made a shrill noise: "Yee, yee, yee ..." and, before my mind had grasped anything, a blur of grey had sped past us. We both banged our bars down with a fearful noise, but, before we'd had time to raise them again, another blur of grey – nearer me – and I could see its frantic gleaming eye – and was mighty glad I had no chance of hitting it. And then, away from us, came a howl and a "Yupee!" and men running about. Someone *had* hit one! And now they were after the animal, jumping on to the rails, and, with a crunching blow and a "Hurray!" they got one. There was silence for a moment as they looked at the corpse. I could imagine it, blood amidst grey. No way was I going to look at it and went back to the bench, which had, as it were, become the RAF man's and my base – I even felt the damp warmth of where I'd sat before.

He came back and grinned at me:

"You should 'ave seen it – a right mess."

I said nothing.

"Now then," he clapped his hands together, looking round him –

"Somewhere must be some food."

"Buffet is closed," I said, "middle of the night."

"That's right," he said, looking round and grinning, "Buffet's closed." He walked around, peering into the insides of the station.

"Come on," he called back to me.

It took courage to refuse for he'd been the only person to take an interest in me, but I was uneasy that he might steal something, so I shook my head.

"Please yourself," he shrugged and disappeared, and I must have dropped off, for the next thing I remember was a blue chocolate bar thrust into my face. He was smiling.

"All yours," he said.

"How did you – ?"

"Ah," he said, his eyebrows going up. "Where there's a will – " I grasped it, tore it open and crunched into the delicious sweetness, and only then did I realise how hungry I was. My stomach could hardly take such a rich diet, but I finished off the bar, thinking this is the only thing to eat before home.

He must have been my guardian angel, for I found myself, through some dreamy vision, on a big train and panicking about missing Nuneaton altogether. Nevertheless, other guardian angels must have put me on Nuneaton station and there stood my local train.

I took a carriage near a station light and saw dust rise from the seat as I flopped down and curled up to keep warm. But warmth was not to be had. The shivering began, and, however tightly I curled myself, it wouldn't stop. 'Sleep, sleep,' I commanded myself, 'you can stand cold in sleep'; and, true, sleep *did* help, and I was awoken by the noise of milk churns being loaded and the welcome sound of someone whistling. And then the train – very, very, slowly – moved, and I slept again, thinking: 'It's the last stage.'

Leicester was heaven, there was no doubt about it. There were *people* there; people walking with purpose, people shouting, people reading newspapers, people banging taxi doors. It was very early – before the yellow-maroon buses had started. I had a choice: to wait, still cold, still astonishingly damp in patches, for a bus (I had just about enough money to get me to Wigston where I lived) or to walk those last five miles. I knew the route for, day in day out, I'd travelled it by bus to school.

So, feeling optimistic, I began the mechanical trudge up the hill to Victoria Park. Don't go too fast, don't slacken when you feel tired – one, two, one two. The park glistened silver/green with early morning dew; then posh Stoneygate – houses well back, gardens immaculate; Oadby reached – there's the cinema which Uncle Doug took me to – all shut now, but still with bright posters; then the last few miles: half suburbs, half country houses.

I didn't think I'd manage the last 100 yards, for half of me didn't want to do them if, at the end, I'd see the dark figure barring the door. I'd rather be back in Wem. No, I wasn't tired any more, all fatigue had vanished. I turned the corner and saw the block of four pretty houses, all painted differently, and there was Uncle Doug's baker's van. I saw him and held back. One look at his face and I'd know. My steps had become a crawl. I edged nearer – he was going into the house and coming out, loading the van -Then he saw me. For a moment I didn't seem to register on his face. Then there came a ferocious grin and I knew, it was OK!

"You'll catch it!" he said, but I knew he liked me, and, that, instead of scolding me, I knew I was a bit of a hero. Mother cried as she hugged me. She kissed me over and over again. "Were you *that* unhappy?" I nodded and added: "Not now that I know you're alive." She hugged me closer and then pushed me away and held me at a distance. "Did you really think I was dead?" Now I felt ashamed of the thought – I saw how ridiculous it was. "Well, I -" and then it burst out: "You never know, do you!" She was silent, trying to control her tears.

Chapter 19

Mr Rowley

Round the corner from the Coopers lived the Rowleys. They were a childless couple who needed money. One night, after I'd crept into mother's bedroom in order to hear her breathing and reassure myself she was alive, she decided I'd be better off with the Rowleys. I'd still be near her but living with another family. She thought it might stop me clinging to her apron strings. It might help me to grow up.

At this time books were the centre of my existence and in them I triumphed at school. But books had no place in the Rowley's household (except Pear's Cyclopaedia) so mine were kept on the sofa where I'd do my homework while Mr Rowley, in the other chair, would rustle his newspaper loudly to disrupt my concentration. Then he'd put the paper down and just glare at me. Was it really a glare or just his normal ugly expression? With bulging eyes like that you couldn't be sure, but it made me feel uncomfortable; in fact, if I wasn't absolutely engrossed in my homework (and who is *all* the time?) I'd shift uncomfortably on the sofa and then did I see a small smile round his thin-lipped mouth? I sensed it rather than saw it for I avoided looking straight at his face if I could help it.

Our battles weren't straightforward, they were oblique and not spoken about – in fact he tried to avoid speech altogether, for in speech I might just get the better of him. He had another battle on with his wife: "You know I can't stand liver," he told her on my first day in the Rowley household. She said bluntly: "I've made it for the lad." There was his plate with its steaming liver and steaming mash and wet dead cabbage and bright orange carrots. She didn't actually say to him: 'Take it or leave it' but simply dumped the plate in front of him, and he ate everything *except* the liver which he ostentatiously left alone – a sign that she wasn't ruling the roost *entirely*. I think it was then that I decided to take her side – she might be unprepossessing in her fat shapelessness, her brisk manner and staccato statements ('Want some custard?' 'You finished?' 'Get on with your homework!') but at least she spoke to me, at least she seemed to care, so I could hardly complain.

At school I was happy, often staying long after it finished by joining the rugger club, the chess club, the debating society – all ways of putting off going home to face his silences and glare. Once home, I'd rush my food and homework and race up to bed.

* * * * *

"What's the capital of New York State?" the question burst unexpectedly into the silence from his thin lips. His eyes had an amused look about them.

"Well, it's not New York that's for sure," I said.

"Come on, come on!" he couldn't wait for me to admit failure.

"Tell you tomorrow ..."

"You don't KNOW!" he was pointing his finger jubilantly at me, his red folds redder than ever, his blue eyes almost out of their sockets. I swallowed my pride.

"No, I don't."

"Albany!" he all but shouted in triumph, and to stop any kind of argument lessening his victory, he quickly picked up the paper, put it high up in front of him as a barrier behind which, no doubt, he gloated.

I couldn't help but smile – it was all so blatant, so obvious: No doubt he was thinking: 'You, the brainy type, don't know everything – so there!' But my pecker was up – no way was I going to get beaten. So, into the school library I went and learnt just about every capital there was. And I'd be subtle about it – ask him casually as if I needed the information for school. So, in an off-hand manner I asked: "By the way, what's the capital of Malaya?"

"Kuala Lumpur," he answered like a shot. 'Good God – he knew!'

"And of Chile?"

"Santiago."

"Bulgaria?"

"Sofia." He knew the lot! I glanced across at Pears' Cyclopaedia where he must have got his information from and he laughed.

"Everything you want in there, boy, don't know why you bother to go to school at all!" Now we were both laughing – the ice had been broken. No, we weren't friends after this, but no longer enemies either. He'd made his point and now, I hoped, the atmosphere in that front room would be a bit less strained.

So why, shortly after that, did he go in for the rat incident? It's always been a puzzle. Perhaps there was something in his nature that thrived on antagonism and he felt positively uncomfortable in a more amiable atmosphere.

"Come out here!" he shouted from the back garden.

"Doing algebra," I called back.

"You come *out*!" it was a bellow, not to be disobeyed.

I went into that horrible unkempt back garden of his; the place was usually cold, wet, muddy with a few sad vegetables in it. He stood in front of something, hiding it from me, and he was smiling.

"Show you something," and he moved aside, and there, looking so innocent, was a grey rat, a small rat, sniffing at the cage wire, long winding tail telling you this *was* a rat and not some cuddly furry pet. It was nervous and occasionally a paw would pick at the firm wire. It shifted its position and I swear looked straight at me in appeal. Being caged was bad enough but nothing to what was about to happen. With a gloved hand he raised the cage, held it high so that it swayed slightly and then held it over a large grey tub full of greenish water. It was his moment of supreme power, and then, slowly, savouring every second, he lowered the cage gradually, very gradually, into the water. The rat retreated into a corner, the water swirled round its paws; it tried to lift them, but inexorably the water rose, engulfed the paws and the lower part of its body, and then the rat, raising its snout into the air, grew frantic, clambered up the side and squealed and squealed until its head was submerged. There was a brief swirl of water and then one large bubble and then some smaller ones; on and on went the bubbles until they lessened and then came one large one and the water calmed and all was still.

He said nothing. He stood at the place of execution and I looked straight at him and knew if I said something he'd call me a 'sissy' and defend himself on the grounds that vermin must be killed. But, I asked myself, 'killed in that sadistic manner? Slowly, savouring the moment, enjoying the power?' I turned and rushed back to my work, but couldn't concentrate: images of the rat appeared, of the bubbles, of Rowley standing there, engrossed. I went upstairs, threw myself on the bed, and thought: 'the man's a monster – I'll never speak another word to him.'

For a time I kept up my silence, but when he tried another ploy: 'What's the longest river in the world, the highest building' and so on, I simply had to answer but showed my reluctance by saying dully 'I don't know' implying I didn't care. He tried another tack:

"You got no hobbies?"

"Yes, I have – I play rugger."

He sneered: "Oh, *rugger* is it? We never played rugger, we played proper football – association football." I tried to ignore his taunts, but then he got up and opened a shiny brown door in the sideboard – one I'd never seen opened before – and he drew out a grey box, opened it carefully and then held it up showing me three beautiful darts. They were white feather type with gleaming golden shafts and enormous long spikes.

"The champion darts," he said proudly.

"Oh."

"I came second in the club championship with these. I tell you, boy, they home in on the double as if they've got minds of their own."

"Show me."

"Not with these – they're for special occasions. He put them carefully back and got out other darts. Then, slowly, ceremoniously, he opened the brown square polished box on the wall behind which he revealed his darts board and proceeded to show me how the game should be played.

"Give me a number up to twenty."

"Sixteen," I said and he aimed, and, after one false shot, got double sixteen. He asked for other numbers and got the double either first or second go. He looked at me in triumph as if to say: 'There you are, *that's* what matters, not your books and all that other rubbish.'

"Can I have a go?" I got up from the sofa.

"Sure," he said.

Of course my first attempts were disastrous, but slowly, very slowly, I got better and, finally, all my three darts scored. No doubt about it, I got a feel for the game.

"Have a go, lad, any time you like," he said generously.

But he was tempting fate for an evil scheme was forming in my mind: 'If I spent hours and hours practising I'd get better and better until one day I'd have his measure.' Of course it was 'evil' because at the darts board he was alive, he was 'at home' there, and every nerve in him went into his arm and eye – here he seemed as near to happiness as he was capable of being and yet I was plotting to beat him.

Quietly, almost secretly, I practised, until, one day, I felt Mrs Rowley standing by my side, watching. She frowned.

"What about your homework?"

"Done it."

"You got any reading to do?"

"No."

"Yes, you have – you've always got books with you – go and get 'em!"

"But Mr Rowley said I could practise any time I wanted ..."

She raised her voice: "I don't care what he said – get on with your reading!"

She was not one to be disobeyed and we both knew what this was about: like me, she sensed there'd come a time when I'd beat her husband, so his self-esteem was at stake and now she was protecting him from the future humiliation. For a second we looked at each other. "Never touch that darts board again – you hear!" And I didn't, and admired her and even liked her for protecting the dignity of her mate.

* * * * *

Then came the day of the great match at the club.

He was dressed in a special way: a brown immaculate suit gave his scrawny body an unusual dignity; the trouser crease was razor sharp, the cut of the jacket perfect in trying to pad out bones that were the minimum to keep body and soul together; the shirt shone in its whiteness, a shiny carmine tie was perfectly tied; the hair, as usual, gleaming and immaculate. He walked by my side with great pride.

"Now you're to sit in the corner and say nothing. I'll get you a lemonade ..."

I smiled.

"You're to watch and nothing else."

"OK."

I'd never before been in the smoky conviviality of a club. They were all 'at home' here and comfortable and on their best behaviour – the bonhomie of folk for whom *this* was their existence, this was where their hearts were – not work, not home, but *here* where the same jokes were repeated and laughed at over-heartily; where you met Joe and asked: "How are things?" And he'd say, "Mustn't grumble," and you thought Joe the greatest guy in the world although you knew that away from the club he was a bastard.

Rowley vanished among the elite, among the team who were all nerves round the dartboard which was lit by a brilliant light. They were the gladiators on whose skill in hand and eye rested the Club's dignity – its pride.

After they'd tossed the coin and shaken hands, they started and I soon realised that among this company Rowley was only just good enough to keep his place. I sensed his nervousness. Outwardly he was very calm, his face showed no emotion; he did his throw, retrieved his darts, said nothing and tried to show nothing. And I also knew that my presence added to his nervousness. In the shadows I might be, hugging my lemonade, now getting warm in my sweaty hands, but he knew I was there.

As numbers went down from 501, he contributed his 50's and 60's, but on the other side was a genius: a small, stocky man with gleaming white shirt and Brylcreemed curly black hair who seemed to be all nerves until arm and eye were perfectly still when he was about to throw. Hardly ever did he score less than 80. I began to fear him for he threw for the 'enemy'. I willed him to miss; I thought he wasn't human, and game after game went to the other side. Soon they were miles ahead and Rowley and cronies looked beaten. Despite their sang-froid, despite the ritual of showing no emotion, you sensed a mental 'giving-up'. "It's that bloody Miller," whispered someone to my left, "he'll do for us." And then something happened! The sinews stiffened, the mind concentrated beyond its normal level, and slowly, slowly our lot began to creep up. 30's became 40's, 50's went to 60 and even 70 and the final double went in almost miraculously. We were on a high: one game, two games, we were catching up, and we did – with one game to go! Teams level. There was hardly a whisper, people had ceased to go to the bar, glasses were left untouched, fists clenched and eyes stared. The final game went down evenly: 436 to them, 424 to us; 261 to them, 252 to us. Now we were ahead – not much – but we'd got our noses in front, and then it was Rowley's turn! If he threw well we'd be in reach of the final double, below the magic 180! Anything could happen. I took a sip of the warm lemonade to wetten my dry throat. His first two darts weren't bad – a score of 52. Now we needed 40 or above. Was it a muscle in his neck that showed the tension? I watched him raise his arm and then from within me a voice rose up and I shouted out: "Come on Mr Rowley!" It didn't entirely stop his throw, not entirely, but there was just the slightest hesitation – the dart flew and went outside the outer rim – a good centimetre from double top. He hadn't done it and I felt a flush of shame. It was me, I'd sabotaged him through willing him to succeed. Would he ever forgive me? The game was lost, the match was lost. 'Close call', 'Good match', 'Well done' went round the teams; the bar was again being used, conversations resumed.

No one told me off, no one said a word to me. Did I imagine angry looks – a curse on the boy who couldn't keep his mouth shut? I looked down at my shoes in humiliation.

He walked in his usual staid fashion. I just hoped to get home without a word being said. Then, as we passed a lit lamppost, I took a sneaky look upward and was taken aback: no, no scowl, no look of anger – I was not to be told off after all.

For two days he brooded on the lost chance and was hardly seen round the house. Then, there he was in the familiar armchair again while I worked. He put his paper down and I looked up at him. But now there was no glare, just a sort of musing look, and then he asked: "You want to come again?"

"Yes, please!" I said eagerly.

"No shouting out this time."

"No, no shouting out," I agreed and we smiled at each other.

Chapter 20

My Bomb

Although I called every adult male I lived with 'Uncle', the only one who played the role with any conviction was Mr Beaumont. He'd ask me over to his place at week-ends and give the Rowley's and mother a rest. I'd be taken into his large, super-polished house, and there – a bit over-awed by all this luxury and by his large florid presence at meals – he'd sit me down, open the Times and ignore me. Nothing else to do, I'd let me dreams go wild and dreamt of cricket glory, for there, just outside the French windows was the large lawn and solid brick wall against which balls could be thrown wildly for practice. If he'd done nothing else, he'd introduced me to the YMCA cricket team. I was taught how to keep score by the senior scorer, while Uncle, looking rather like some large white tent, would umpire in the middle. A no-nonsense umpire – finger raised instantly, flamboyant flourish for a boundary, raised leg for a leg-bye. You didn't argue with Uncle. He was 'in charge' and loved every minute of it, and, going home, he'd go through the game with a love of detail which, in turn, roused ambition in me.

I suppose he was the nearest I had to a dad, so I always wanted him to be 'in charge'. For instance, I loved it when, with great pomp and ceremony, he took me to civic functions, where, a general big-wig he would exchange hearty greetings with other big-wigs while I gobbled up the goodies and looked at the city's high and mighty. "You'll meet Alderman Keene," he said, "our next Lord Mayor, and if you see a man with bright Brylcreemed hair that'll be Dr Thomas – best education officer we ever had." And his little blue eyes would twinkle, and I knew, for better or worse, I'd become the son he never had and I was quite happy with that, for, apart from Rowley, I needed a man around – one who could occasionally even be nasty and mischievous. Sometimes he'd drive up to an old lady crossing the road gingerly and give a big blast on his car horn. She'd jump, poor dear, look at us all startled and scuttle across. 'No', I thought, 'he's not a nice man, but who cares for '*nice* men' – I'd rather have a bit of a devil – someone who frightens old ladies and is pompous and knows his way around'. Also, I think, I first saw in him the many sided facets of human nature. For instance, he would cry his way through the film 'Brief Encounter' (so would I) and then, ashamed of showing weakness, he'd growl and nag at me. I couldn't love him for there was something unlovable in him, but I could respect and emulate and enjoy what he enjoyed – pomp and sport, and, besides, every week-end; there was a treat of some sort.

One Friday evening he said – very gravely – "We're fire-watching tonight, and we're doing it on *my* building." *His* building was the large YMCA in Leicester with its huge roof where fire-bombs could lurk and ignite much later. It needed watching and I got excited. "Do we sleep there?" "Oh, yes, it's at night that the devils come." We prepared: sandwiches and a thermos. "Don't need blankets, they've got plenty. Now listen, when the sirens go you get up and join me." In the centre of the building was a grand circular staircase and I looked up at the ceiling and thought: 'If a bomb drops right I jump left and vice versa.' I felt the energy of fight in me and thought: 'They won't get me.'

I was awakened rudely in my little cubby hole: "Come on, they're coming." I jumped up in excitement. "Up the roof!" he said, and up the roof we went. What a Mars-like landscape that was, full of shadowy greys and blacks and drain pipes over which you could trip. Gingerly we ambled along and there to our right was a large orange glow. Other men now joined us. "They hit the parcels office near the station, bastards," said one. "No need for that language!" said my Uncle sternly and the man looked rebuked. But the glow was very bright and we all looked and knew that's where the fire-engines were and the police and ARP and we felt strangely vulnerable. "What happens if another one comes?" "We'll deal with it," said a chirpy-like cockney lad. 'Dealing with it' meant stirrup pumps – quaint double steel bars, one handle and a bucket of water. 'Little good that'll do,' I thought, 'Never mind, we'll deal with it, somehow.' We looked, searching for those two-feet grey tubes that meant fire-bombs, and, disappointed, no one found one. So we drifted downstairs and stood in the street and stared at where the action was. "Seem to know what to hit," said one man appreciatively. "Bastards," said another, but, this time, Uncle said nothing. No one knew what to do. "If they try it again who do we call first, the police or the fire-brigade? They're all too busy at the station."

Bored, I crossed the narrow street and went to the waste-ground opposite. All hollows and hills – an eye-sore which no one knew what to do with and had been around for years. I wandered about thinking what a splendid playground *this* would make, and then I noticed a difference in the earth; most of the hills and hollows were hardened by the sun, but there was a circular soft bit, and, picking up a bit of earth, I thought: 'That's been done recently' – it was in the shape of an inverted cone with something at the bottom – something gleaming. I peered and peered. Surely not! Someone would have checked, and if there was a bomb down there they'd have heard something. 'No, they wouldn't,' I thought, for it had plummeted into soft earth. I recalled the rumour about land-mines dropped by parachute – one had fallen plumb on the Victoria Pavilion and everyone laughed. "Wanted to get rid of that horrible eye-sore for years – now the sporty lot will have to change in the open air; we'll be able to watch the women!" I went cautiously down the volcano-like hole, and, yes, something *was* gleaming: I'd found a bomb! I was absolutely delighted! I raced across the road to the knot of men and shouted: "Over there- there's a bomb!" But they ignored me – they were still debating who to call first and a fierce argument had developed so who cares for a youngster who's fantasizing! "Down there – there's a crater – *I tell you there's a bomb*!" But Uncle had turned his back on me and I couldn't even get his attention, never mind the others. I didn't know what to do – never had I felt so helpless in the face of adult indifference. They were completely absorbed in their argument. I sensed the thing might go off: a time-bomb, after all, is *timed*. I rushed round the circle of men. "Over there!" I pointed. But it was no good, so I gave up. If they took no notice of me perhaps I *was* fantasizing! So I went back, and, true enough, there it lay, innocently, steel at the bottom of a crater. It was then that Uncle called me: "Come back!" he shouted. I pointed, "Look!" Something in my urgency must have warned him. He came across rather slowly – never lose your dignity – and he peered down. "Can't see anything." "Down there – a steely thing. Look, the earth's fresh." He turned back towards the men and went over the road to speak to them. They rushed across and stood in a circle round the crater, their faces white in the dark. "*Looks* like a bomb," said one, "Ring the ARP." Then one of them panicked: "Get out of here – it's a timer!" and I've never seen men move faster. But I stood there and felt proud. 'My bomb – it's mine – *I* found it.'

I don't know how they defused it, but it caused no harm. However, the crater stood for a long while before the earth, under the impress of wind and weather, changed to look like the earth around it. But, as far as I know, the crater is still there, and, every time I pass it on a bus, I feel immensely proud. 'It's *my* bomb – they should put up a plaque.'

Chapter 21

Uncle

I got on so well with Uncle Beaumont that mother asked me if I wanted to leave the Rowleys and stay with him permanently. I said 'yes' without hesitation, because I felt Mr Beaumont could teach me so much more – his world a wider and richer one than the Rowleys'.

So there I was in his large garden practising catching a ball by banging it against the wall, when I noticed a woman's eyes because they were the only still point among the ever-moving trees behind her. They were grey eyes motionless among a halo of grey curls. Who was she? What was she doing out here? Possibly thinking: 'That boy's no good, never make the school team,' or, perhaps she was a ghost? I laughed at my fancy and then had an even more fanciful thought – she *liked* watching me, got a thrill out of seeing a young body hurl about; perhaps she liked my muscles, and, with that thought uppermost, I began to exaggerate my movements – leaping into the air (like a tiger I imagined) to catch the high ones. And then, when I took a peep to see her reactions, I saw only the swaying trees – she'd gone.

No, I would not tell Uncle about her. She would be a part of that private life I needed to carve out for myself in the all-male duo in which we lived. It was a shared life in which I did the drying up and tidied my room, and, every week, was solemnly handed a duster to do the wooden bits by the side of the grey stair carpet. Another job was handing him the plates from high up in the kitchen – because the man was too portly (a polite way of putting it) to get them down himself. 'Arthritis' he grumbled, and I sensed his envy at my athleticism, my quick movements, my pounding up the stairs, and I wasn't beyond 'showing off' even on our cricket outings where he was very much 'the boss'.

I don't think I was ever aware of how limited his life was. His wife was away looking after an ill mother, and his grown-up daughter, Marianne, was in the WRENS. In the evening he would read or put the wireless on for the news or a comedy (usually Tommy Handley). To me, that seemed to be the sum of his life. If I hadn't been so engrossed in myself, I'd have been more conscious of his loneliness. As it was, I sensed it occasionally, but didn't let it worry me, until, that is, he went moody and would glower at everything, including me. Then the house's habitual silence became positively threatening. At first his bad moods got to me, but the resilience of boyhood and the realisation that I was king (or at least crown prince) in this domain gave me a sort of physical freedom that lifted my spirits. Anyway, as I got to know Uncle better and sensed he welcomed my presence, I surmounted the place's gloom and filled it with my thoughts. And sometimes, to cheer myself up, I would take a peep into the understairs cricket cupboard. Here was *real* life! Pads frayed at the edges, old white trousers with green smudges still on, scarred wickets, balls often squashed like plums, and, of course, bats battle-scarred, sometimes even split – all the repository of dreams. The cupboard was filled to the brim, so if you opened it something nearly always fell out. This time it was a wicket-keeper's glove. I was impressed:

"*You* kept wicket?"

"Sometimes," he said, unable to disguise his pride.

"Always in the middle of the action," I grinned.

"Always" he said, and then, after a pause: "Put it on."

"What?"

"The glove – put it on."

I hesitated, and then plunged my hand into its hugeness where it got completely lost. We both laughed.

"Got a lot of growing to do," he said.

"Yes."

"But you're coming on fast. Let me feel your biceps."

"What's that?"

"Here."

And he felt my upper arm.

"My – " he said, "You'll be a strong lad in time."

And then, as though he'd over-stepped some barrier, he hurried away. I felt the impress of his fingers on my arm and realised this was the first time he'd ever touched me and also felt proud of his verdict: "A strong lad, eh!" And, later, in return for his praise and helped by the air of intimacy that had developed, I decided to tell him about the mysterious woman next-door.

"I thought she was a ghost," I laughed, and went on: "Who is she?"

"Miss Pickering," and then added darkly: "Note – *Miss*."

I nodded sagely, though not sure what he was getting at.

"Spinsters," he said, leaning back in his chair, "can go peculiar through loneliness."

Then he smiled at me. "So she's been watching you, has she?"

"Yes."

"Perhaps," he grinned broadly, "she *likes* watching you – enjoys it."

I looked down at my toast in embarrassment. He paused for a second and I sensed his eyes were fully on me:

"Sex," he blurted out, "What do you know about it?"

I didn't look up.

"Embarrassed are you?" he chuckled.

I said nothing, though he was right – I'd only picked up this and that in my all-boys school where fantasy reigned and facts were in short supply.

"We must have a talk," he said. And, without further ado, he placed me in his huge armchair, and, with the sun shining full in my face so there was no way I could avoid his scrutiny, he asked:

"Now then, you noticed any changes recently?"

"Sorry I don't know what you mean."

"Changes, lad, you know, on your body?"

"On my body?"

"Well, shall we say –"

(And I swear he blushed)

"Hair – you know –" he didn't seem to know how to go on, "Hair –" he repeated. I looked down, unable to say a word.

"Well," he became hearty, "happens at your time of life – Now, nothing to worry about – nothing at all –"

I thought I was about to be dismissed and was ready to make a dash for it, but then his voice altered to a matter-of-fact one – a dull lecturer's voice – and he gave me a mercilessly detailed account of *all* the male changes including things 'popping up', and excretions that were 'nothing to worry about'. I tried not to listen to this reduction of something intimately private into a matter-of-fact biological world which seemed to have no link whatever to what was really happening to me. The relaxation, the dreams, the ecstasy – all ignored, and, did I now hear right? – he'd switched to girls. Oh heavens, what had all this to do with girls – those aliens who were (I wasn't quite sure how) differently constructed – and here 'tubes' and 'eggs', and then, as the sweat on my brow increased, the word 'blood' sent my temples thumping. I thought I'll pass out – but no, I jumped up and raced for the bathroom.

He came after me and began fussing round and I sensed he wanted to touch me, to comfort me in some way. I watched the dribble of brown from my mouth go into the washbasin and heaved exaggeratedly as he fussed round me.

"It's OK, old chap. Nothing to worry about –"

Don't say that! It's everything to worry about – it's so very much my own thing and should have remained so – no, it's nothing to do with 'eggs' and 'blood' – anyway, what was I to *do* about it? That was the question – not *not* do, but *do*?

At bedtime he knocked timidly at my door, "Can I come in?"

Except to check its tidiness, he rarely intruded.

"Yes," I said and saw the concern in his eyes. His huge bulk leant over me as I lay in my pyjamas in bed; and then he sat down and the bed tilted heavily to his side.

"You feeling any better?"

"I'm fine," I tried to sound jaunty.

"Brought you some water," and he put the glass carefully down on my bedside table.

"Thanks," I said, and, as I saw real anxiety in his eyes, I think I grew rather fond of him.

Suddenly he jumped up. "Come on, you need a bit of comfort. Get up! Come one, come on …"

"But where – ?"

"Into the big bedroom."

That was *his* bedroom. But by now he'd torn the blankets off me and cajoled me into getting up. So, shivering, I went down the corridor and stood outside the big bedroom, looking in. I hesitated. There was his huge bed.

"That's your side," he said, indicating the left. I just stood there.

"Come on then, " he said, "get in." And I did, glad of the bed's warmth.

I turned my face away from him so that I heard, but didn't see, him getting undressed. Then there was the tilt of the bed as he got in. For a while there was silence.

"You feeling better?" he asked.

"Yes, thank you," I said very politely.

Again silence.

Then slowly, very slowly, I sensed his hand moving towards me. I lay quite still; every now and then his hand would stop then start again. When he got uncomfortably close, I tuned ostentatiously away and buried my head in the pillow. Quickly his hand retreated. There was a pause. Then he tried again – once more the hand came creeping, but this time I was determined to show him how unwelcome his groping was – my turning away was definite – it said 'no'.

'What on earth do we say in the morning?' I thought. 'How do we face each other?' I didn't want to embarrass him and decided that the only policy was to say nothing; to pretend none of this had happened and go on as before. And then I fell asleep.

I was lucky in the morning for there, on the table, was a very grand-looking letter which took all our attention. It was a yellow letter with a crest on it. He seemed to hesitate before opening it. Then, with a knife he did open it. I was watching him out of the corner of my eye. He read it and laid it down.

"A JP," he muttered.

"What?"

"Justice of the Peace – a magistrate – they've asked me to be one."

I asked: "What do you do?"

He smiled, "We pass judgement on our fellow-men."

I dug into my egg.

"That's scary," I said.

"Is it?" he was half smiling.

"Yes, you may get it wrong."

"We may indeed." He began to score the tablecloth with his knife.

"Celebrate!" he said suddenly, "We must celebrate! Come on – you've finished your breakfast – " And he got behind my chair and pulled it backwards.

"Eh -!" I shouted, laughing.

"Outside we go and I'll show you what real catching is!" And before I could say anything, he'd opened the French window to be greeted by the welcoming sun. I got hold of the tennis ball when he said with contempt. "Ah, this piss-pot of a ball! Go inside, lad, and get a real one!"

A real cricket ball! The thought was slightly intimidating – a real cricket ball can hurt if it hits the end of your fingers. But, I realised, this was real man's stuff now. Uncle's face became very red as he threw as hard as he could; his little blue veins throbbed away and he sweated and puffed as he tried to outdo my agility. It became a contest of age versus youth, and in the middle of it suddenly I saw the face by the trees, and, as Uncle and I crashed against each other, I whispered, "She's there!"

"I know," he said and winked.

"Right," he said loudly so she would hear, "I'll show you how to do the googly."

"Already?" I was overawed. The googly was the ultimate in human deception and skill.

"You're good enough. Come on."

And with his enormous arms around me, he put my fingers in the right position on the ball, and then with the twist of the wrist the batsman mustn't see, I sort of managed one. He did this several times, and then, as if an imp had got into him, he called out loudly, "Don't let the ball crash against Miss Pickering's fence, will you!"

I protested, "But I never – "

"Shush," he put his finger on his lips and winked again and then shouted loudly; "We must be neighbourly, get on with each other!"

I looked anxiously towards the fence and the face had vanished. We looked at each other and laughed and laughed. We went inside still laughing and were very happy; the night's incident might never have happened.

Two days later a crumpled white letter appeared on the doormat – no stamp on, it had been pushed through our snapping letter-box and got torn. Of course we knew who it was from.

"Anything interesting?" I asked.

"Shouldn't think so," he said, and then, as if handling a dirty object, he tore it open. I waited and then he exploded: "Of all the bloody cheek! Who the hell does she think she is – !" And he got up and left the room. All I had to do was lean over a bit to read what was in the letter. And was just about doing so, catching the words 'indecent' 'boy alone' when he came back, swept up the letter, bunched it into his pocket and left again.

The next few days were awful. He was in a foul mood and I could do nothing right:

"Plate!" he shouted with his apron on.

I reached for one.

"Not that one, stupid, you don't put toast on a dinner plate!"

"Sorry."

When he was in that mood, silence was the best weapon. But I ached for him to talk properly – confide in me – surely I was old enough. That day, coming home from school, I saw him sitting in his chair and looking like I'd never seen him before; he was crumpled – even seemed smaller; his head bowed, hands clenched, he couldn't meet my eyes and talked as if to the floor:

"Bloody done for me. Got this letter today." He held it up. "'A complaint' they said – 'must investigate – not invited to the Bench yet –'"

"Well – " I began, "perhaps they'll change their minds -"

"It means never!" he shouted at me and looked as if I was the enemy. "Have I done anything to you – ?" and stopped. Then he looked down again and half mumbled: "Not your fault, boy, not your fault." And then, suddenly, he banged his hands on his knees, got up and rushed out through the hall, opened the front door, went out and banged it shut behind him. I raced upstairs and went into my room where the window looked out on to the front and there he was determinedly marching up Miss Pickering's concrete path. 'Bang, bang, bang' went the shiny brass knocker on her front door. Surely she wouldn't come out, she wouldn't dare – she'd shy away after seeing his large frame through the glass. But the door *did* open and not cautiously either but brazenly, and there she was, smaller than he but erect, ready to do battle. I couldn't hear what he said, but saw his jaw snapping away. However, she didn't give an inch, and then, to my surprise, she answered back – a few words at first and then a torrent and now one could see her anger, her fury. So there they were slanging each other, and then, suddenly, she stepped back and banged the door in his face, his nose could only have been an inch from the green woodwork. He stood there panting for a moment, undecided, confused. Slowly, he turned away, still looking as if he was throbbing with anger, but I could see he was thinking. His head was down.

He'd gone out without his keys so I had to open the door. He ignored my look and went upstairs and stopped there for hours until I began to worry.

"Want a cup of tea?" I shouted up – but no answer.

He was an awful long time up there and when he did come down he was in a subdued mood. I simply daren't ask a thing and hoped that, somehow, in time, this would all pass.

Well, it did pass, but not back to normal. After the Pickering battle our lives changed as Uncle became mysteriously busy. There were 'phone calls' he took strictly in private, he went out a lot by himself. 'Dinner needs warming' notes left on the table and once there was a visit by a lady ushered into the front room away from my ears and sight. Dread began to fill me – I think I knew what was going on, but, by not asking, hoped it would all go away. Once I sought solace by going into the garden for a bit of solitary throwing, but it was listless, and as for the googly – hopeless. I got fed up with this and then glanced towards the trees, and, yes, there was the face. I picked up the ball, the *real* ball and bounced it thoughtfully up and down as if deciding what to do with it, and then, suddenly, I threw it – no, I didn't hurl it, just an arc and one that went nowhere near her, but it was enough for the face to darken and disappear.

“Bitch!” I muttered, and wished I’d have really thrown it at her – I wouldn’t have missed!

* * * * *

He called me as I passed his bedroom. “Come in, will you.”

I did.

He was in bed, his small eyes larger than usual.

“Sit down,” he patted the space by his side. I did, rather hesitantly.

“You been happy here?”

I nodded, not absolutely sure one way or the other.

“Good,” he said, “Yes, I’ve been happy to have you here. However,” he sighed, “While your mother comes to see you every now and then, a boy needs a woman around all the time.” He paused.

“What do you think?”

“Don’t know,” I mumbled.

“Oh, yes he does. In a way they’re right – quite right. So – ” he paused again.

“You’ll be going to a nice couple not far from here. I’ve been to see them.”

The thought of change yet again was quite awful. I thought I’d found somewhere permanent.

“Why?” I mumbled, tears not far away, for I’d grown fond of him.

“Because – “ he hesitated and then turned his face away. I saw only his red pate and the semi-circle of grey hair, and his words barely reached me:

“Because you’re becoming too beautiful.”

Chapter 22

Marianne

Although no longer living with Uncle, we kept in contact, and, as before, I'd spend week-ends in his home. We'd become good companions, with sport as the 'binding factor'.

Gradually the house changed: his wife re-appeared having looked after her mother, and then his WREN daughter returned, creating a completely different atmosphere in the place. It wasn't long before I had a crush on Marianne.

I couldn't see her head for it was completely immersed in the sports cupboard beneath the stairs. Her breasts hung down, her dark navy-blue hockey get-up covered her down to her thighs and beneath were white muscular legs that must have withstood many a knock from foreign hockey sticks. Such a firm muscular being yet Marianne was every inch a woman! She withdrew her head and never before had the brilliant redness of her hair struck me so forcefully – it seemed as if her white freckled face was on fire. For a fraction of a second she looked puzzled at my staring at her, then her features contorted into a mask of contempt. She must have recognised the mixture of lust and awe in my face; she came forward, hockey stick raised aggressively, and made straight towards me so I had to give way as she brushed rudely past me. I didn't mind the brief contemptuous shoulder contact, in fact, I treasured it for rarely in that inhibited household had anyone ever made physical contact with me. We were a no-touch group of people – her father, mother, Marianne and me; a Puritan household if ever there was one.

Was I right in thinking that she hated me as only a twenty year old sporty girl can hate a thirteen year old bookish intruder: an adolescent boy going through the turmoil of puberty, ever casting covetous glances at her, who drank in every movement of her body, who she had to stare at over the marmalade dish at breakfast, who, through a wish to gain attention, wouldn't pass that dish when she asked for it and who'd stare with envy when her friends called for her with their raucous voices and repellent heartiness.

Yet when she left that house for hockey, the place seemed very empty. No noise, no bustle, no shout of: "I can't find my blue sweater, mum. I *know* I put it in my top drawer."

Her mother, a resigned ghost, with ever a gentle smile, would quietly show her where the elusive sweater was, and, sometimes, would also ask me: "What are you going to do today, Jackie?"

"Play cricket," I'd reply, knowing I was expected to say that, for sport was the only respectable activity in that house. Inactivity was looked at askance for all were aware of hormones buzzing dangerously away in young frames, hormones that inevitably led to visions which might find temporary relief in a lonely bed; hormones that had to be suppressed at all costs!

Uncle drew three wickets with chalk on the brick wall.

"Now this is about twenty two yards," he measured out, "and here – " he placed a handkerchief on the lawn, "is your target. It's what's called a length."

We loved these times together. I sweated my guts out, felt a thrill every time I hit the handkerchief, got better and better, and thought that, with application, yes, I might, just might, make the House Team. And one day, by golly, I did! There it was on the drawing-pin studded, black notice-board, under the heading 'Charnwood House' – there was *my* name!

"I'm in the House Team," I muttered shyly at breakfast (one mustn't show-off! Never boast – never praise yourself!) But all eyes were on me. Uncle positively expanded his huge frame, Aunt actually brought her features into a *real* smile and even Marianne, for ever engrossed in thoughts of sporting heroics, actually gave me a glance, and in that quick look I saw the extraordinary light blueness of her eyes. Strange, I'd never seen those eyes quite like that before – what purity – what sheer blueness, and I thought: 'I'd lay my life down for you. All I ever really want is to be noticed by you – to become a shard of consciousness in that ever-busy brain, to become someone you would, very, very occasionally, *think* about.' Now, for a moment, she *was* thinking about me. But not for long, soon her perfect white teeth sank into a crunchy sweet mixture of marmalade, running butter and crispy toast.

I made a pig of myself at that breakfast as a private reward for making the House Team, and, although I felt indigestion coming on, I went outside and with a real cricket ball peppered the wall with ferocity – never mind the handkerchief – no handkerchiefs during a real match. I bowled like a demon, and then, looking up, saw Uncle, and the heavens be praised – Marianne staring at me, and for the first time in our relationship she was smiling at me. I tried hard to get a reciprocal smile on my face – oh, I tried, but before the gaze of angels one is struck immobile, and then the smile left her face and she returned into the blackness of the lounge. No knight in shining armour has felt more beholden to his lady than I did at that moment, and promptly, with even greater gusto, I continued to bowl, but the ball was now going all over the place.

Uncle padded towards me – his great bulk now a beaming human being, and gently, behind me, his stomach in the small of my back, he took hold of my right arm with his and showed me how to get the rhythm of keeping a length. Very gradually our bodies moved in unison, in complete harmony. Then he stepped back, and was puffing so much that he was hardly able to say: "Good lad, keep it up!" Then, to my surprise, he got hold of my shoulder and gave it a squeeze, a squeeze I sensed was saying 'Thank you', or perhaps more than 'Thank you'.

* * * * *

Barely had the postman's rattle stopped when Marianne rushed into the hall. She came back with a blue letter in her hand already almost half torn open, her fingers barely able to keep up with her impatience. She took the letter out of its envelope and read the precious words – head moving back and forth. We could tell it was good news by the smallest of smiles. She sat down and sighed and said, barely audibly, "He's coming on leave." Her mother gave the warmest of smiles and her father looked as pleased as he could manage.

"When?" he asked.

"Next Saturday."

"Better get the champers out." But she wasn't listening – she was dreaming – of what? I could guess, but marvelled at such uninhibited happiness, while, of course, being fiercely jealous. 'Lucky man' I thought. I hoped he'd be some shrunken soldier in ill-fitting uniform, or, at worst, a sergeant or something, but knew it was unlikely. Marianne's lover would be out of a romantic novel – there'd be gold braid on his sleeve (I'd discovered he was in the navy), he'd have far-away looking blue eyes – there'd be golden curls and a strong muscular body. He'd have a low male voice – a bass accompaniment to her merry tinkle, and he'd be every way both suitable and desirable.

He was. I got everything right except that his golden curls were wispy light-brown hair and his eyes were deep, serious-looking brown. The gold braid was more than I could stand – two broad stripes and a thin one between – a lieutenant commander! He seemed so young that his rank was even more impressive. His body was muscular all right, and, seen in tennis shorts, his sturdy brown legs were like solid columns. A sporty type and yet – was there no end to this man's accomplishments? – he was also a language scholar – versed in French and Latin. This was the bitterest blow for I imagined intellectual achievements to be my preserve – it was the counter-balance to all this sweaty sportiness, for, house team or no, I realised I could never aspire to that absorption in muscular activity which dominated Marianne's (and now Maurice's) lives. I may be competent at bowling a length, but they were good at *all* sports. Nor was this the end of Maurice's virtues for he was diffident and quiet and dominated the breakfast conversation by the simple expedient of answering eager questions from Marianne and her adoring parents. My envy knew no bounds. Marianne sat there quietly eating, basking in the reflected glory of 'her man' and giving him every chance to shine. Then she whispered something in his ear, getting as close as was polite in public, and he blushed:

"No, no" he said.

"Yes, yes," she replied, and announced in unashamed pride:

"He's getting a medal!"

"No!" said Mrs Beaumont in astonishment.

Mr Beaumont leant back in his chair, eyes twinkling, but did I discern just the merest shade of envy in his demeanour?

"Come on, tell all," said Mr Beaumont. And Maurice talked, with as much modesty as he could muster, of rescuing a German airman in Arctic conditions.

It was too much! Could there be a man with *all* God's gifts on his shoulders? Can the earth produce heroes of such stature, who had looks, courage, intelligence, health *and* Marianne.

It seems it could and even the weather was casting a benediction on them for the sun shone on this glorious pair as they romped up and down stairs as though the earth belonged to them (perhaps it did).

"Today I'm practising my back hand," he told his darling.

"You certainly need *some* practice," she said, giggling at this innuendo, and there were smothered cuddles, more giggles and I could only imagine what intimacies on the stairs.

Apart from spying on them, I tried to disappear and glean what comfort I could from Thomas Hardy's short stories. The savour had gone out of bowling at a wall and the house match had been no great event so I didn't mention it, in fact, I mentioned hardly anything, for in their eyes, especially Marianne's, I wasn't there. I wasn't even a ghost (for ghosts are memorable), I'd never seen a woman so glowing, so active, so self-absorbed.

To distance them was my only hope, not easy in a house which was full of them. And then the bond I sensed with Mr Beaumont bore fruit. As if divining my isolation, my envy, my secret passion, he came into the library room as I sat, half disconsolate, half bored, with only a book for company, and there, ostentatiously between his legs was a cricket bat – a huge thing, much pitted and scarred.

"It's mine," he said, "I used it in my glory days." He gave a rueful smile, "a long time ago." I said nothing, though guessing what he was about to do.

"You have it," he said, pushing it forward. "Take some getting used to – a bit big for you. Never mind, day by day you're growing. Let's feel your muscles." He leant forward and felt, kneading my thin sinews.

"You'll do," he said and got up, and, with a catch in his voice, he said: "Remember, you're growing, day by day. Soon you'll be – " he didn't finish his sentence and left and I sensed his kindness. I felt very warm towards him.

But the only real consolation was that, sooner or later, Maurice would have to go back to the navy. When the time came it was turmoil. Marianne was inconsolable as Maurice, grimly silent, packed. She cried openly, she stormed at the injustice of war; she kissed and cuddled him brazenly at the front door when he was about to leave. He went, she turned, rushed up the stairs and, all over the house, we could hear her sobs.

The place returned to silence as Marianne, red-eyed, merely grunted at breakfast. The only time she came alive was when she heard the news on the brown bakelite radio. She listened with anguish for the word 'Portsmouth', for, breaking regulations, he'd told her that's where he'd be.

"Bombing on the London area. On Coventry, on Liverpool, on Glasgow ..."

We all knew what *she* was listening for, and then it came:

"Some southern coastal towns were hit last night. Three enemy aircraft ..."

There was an awesome silence. Southern coastal towns? There were so many of them! But she was seriously disturbed, she fidgeted with her toast, she could barely keep still, and then our eyes met and I saw hatred: 'Why wasn't I Maurice? What a horrible object I was!' and then, unable to stop myself, I heard myself say: "Perhaps it was Portsmouth."

Without a word she left breakfast and raced upstairs. The three of us continued, unable to meet each other's eyes. Then, finding this beyond me, I pushed back my chair and rushed into the library room – my only sanctuary. Why, why, why? I felt tears approaching, but choked them back. How could I – ? I sensed her anguish, there was nothing I wouldn't do to console her, but felt helpless. What must she be thinking – the whine of bombs, crumbling buildings and her darling – ! I knew it had been revenge for weeks of isolation and the suppressed passion of a half-formed youth. I also knew it was unforgivable – a black spot I'd have to bear for the rest of my life.

Chapter 23

Finding Father

At school small Pringle came up to me and asked: "Is Alster a common name?"

I said "No."

"Well," continued Pringle, "there's an Alster on the cover of this week's Picture Post," and he was off, chasing a ball. Picture Post was our eyes on the world in those pre-TV days, and, lo and behold, there was a picture of my father; a little fatter, cigar as usual in his mouth and looking as handsome as ever.

His story was out of John Buchan or Anthony Hope – he'd walked, yes, *walked*, across the Alps, handed himself over to the Italians and spent the war (quite well if the picture was anything to go by) in an internment camp near Milan. The Italians seemed to shrug their shoulders at the appearance of such strangers, and he met no anti-Semitism. End of the war, and Canadians attached to the 8th Army, through a gesture of good-will, allowed a hundred refugees to go over to Canada. Of course dad, with his luck, was one of them. He'd not only survived Hitler, but now we'd found him.

Mother could hardly contain herself. To find his address, she wrote off everywhere, and there, one day, lay a blue airmail letter on the doormat. He told us his marriage to Rosa had broken up, and would she (mother) re-marry him? She gulped, giggled and blushed at the implications. Then brooded long and hard and said "No." Why? I never found out. Did the thought of moving yet again to another country over-awe her? Was she involved with another man? I don't know, but she said, "Sorry and all that, but …" Father, unshaken, made his way to the New York Jewish Community, where he met a very charming lady and married her. It was his third marriage.

For a short time it was happy and he wrote to me: 'What did I want for my birthday?' I asked for Ibsen's plays. I got them and they were promptly stolen. So now I have no record of father's handwriting and I curse the thief. Not long afterwards, father died of lung cancer – all those cigars!

My mother survived long enough to enjoy some kind of peace and a new life for herself. She died in 1989 at the age of 89 – her own story still largely untold.

Uncle Norbert (he who had been so cruel to his father by ignoring him) also re-appeared – a successful architect in New York, he got married, we exchanged a couple of letters, and then, sadly, he also died.

So, about half the family survived, and half perished in the Holocaust. I don't know whether you call that lucky or not.

But, of course, for me it had all broken up. Instead of growing up an orthodox, Bah-mitzvahed Jew, I had become a secular being, who had absorbed an alien culture, and hardly considered himself as belonging anywhere at all. Of course all the people I'd lived with influenced me. I'd crossed and re-crossed the English class system; I'd met cruelty, envy and stupidity as well as kindness, warmth and generosity. Those who looked after me faced no easy task. My insecurity made me very demanding, my temperament was unstable, and the only constant in my life being mother, I was terrified of losing her.

How badly I missed my father I was not aware of until I noticed that even in maturity I responded to men-friends in a child-father manner. Often this put a strain on what might otherwise have been a healthy and fruitful relationship.

Let no one under-estimate the presence of an adult male in the family. As the only child of divorced parents, I felt his absence keenly. In particular, he'd left me vulnerable to the terror that if anything happened to mum I was alone in the world – a source of nightmares. There was another factor: I had no model as to how to be a father myself. When my two sons were born, I was caught between over-strictness and laxity. The attitude of the time was to be 'mates' with your sons, so I played football with them and taught them chess – but this was all easy stuff, the rest was left to their mother and it is to her credit that they haven't turned out too badly. Nevertheless, there were quite a few moments when the three of them laughed and joked and I felt the outsider – I envied their intimacy. I believe this to be fairly common with fathers.

Several times I badly wanted to convey to them the warmth and character of the ghetto – I wanted a shared experience and hoped they'd become aware of their heritage. But how could they? We were a secular family of mixed religious backgrounds. It would have been hypocrisy to impose any religion on them, so, regrettably, we left things to chance.

But there were advantages in my nomadic and chaotic experience. I grew to accept a very wide spectrum of humanity and thereby developed a tolerance of all types – a sort of 'a man's a man for a that' attitude. For instance I was able to become friendly with a cramped and sadistic personality like Rowley and could handle Uncle Beaumont's suppressed homosexuality without giving him pain. I even liked dance-obsessed Hilda while a kind of love developed between Uncle Doug and myself. Life was very rich – the world full of interest, and, add to that an eager response to literature, by way of dear Mr George, and, whatever insecurities lay beneath, there was a fair amount of happiness. I was probably as content as most children.

Now, in my 70's, I have become a member of my local Jewish Community. I am not very conscientious or active, but I belong. During services I respond to the shawl and kippah, I like the rhythms and 'music' of Hebrew without understanding a word. Folk memories stir, ghosts of the past move me, I can hear the sounds of the ghetto again.

Many do not make this long and unmapped journey towards finding an identity. But, like me, they inter-marry and so the number of Jews in the Diaspora is diminishing. It is argued they are doing Hitler's work and 'solving' the Jewish question in their own way. Why, after going down this route for so long, have I returned to the fold? The proximity of death has something to do with it – I won't deny that – but really it's the recognition that however secular in thought and deed I have become, I am unquestionably – and, yes, proudly – still a Jew.

PhD graduation day, with mother looking very frail

Father fit and healthy in New York